END OF THE VINE

A DANIEL WINTERS MYSTERY

ACTON MANNING

CONTENTS

Copyright

Prologue: Eden Hope

1. A Distorted Crowd
2. The Nagging Note
3. Splitting at the Seams
4. Birth and Death
5. Kristin's World
6. Downtown Heart
7. On the Lees
8. Stormy Night
9. Too Late to See Leroy
10. Nagging Note Revisited
11. Ghosts of Richebourg
12. Blood Red Lips
13. Paid Vacation
14. My Only Father
15. Bon Appétit
16. Bittersweet

Also by Acton Manning

Sign Up Now!

About the Author

Copyright © Acton Manning, 2022

All rights reserved. No part of this book may be reproduced or used in any manner without the prior written permission of the copyright owner, except for the use of brief quotations in a book review.

This is a work of fiction. Any resemblance to persons living or deceased is purely coincidental.

Paperback ISBN: 979-8-9861755-7-7

E-book ISBN: 979-8-9861755-0-8

Cover art: Pinguino Kolb

Editor: Arlene Prunkl, Penultimate Editing

Copy editor: Lynne Melcombe Communications

Published by YFB Publishing

Website: www.actonmanning.com

Email: acton.manning@gmail.com

Twitter: @ActonManning

Facebook: Acton Manning

Created with **Vellum**

PROLOGUE: EDEN HOPE

Moonlight and shadow splashed over the eerie landscape of the Eden Hope playground. The merry-go-round groaned softly as it circled in a placid breeze. Rainbow-striped metal bars arched over a cracked foam strip, waiting for children to grip them and swing from one to the next. But no children were here now. No one was here. It was almost ten o'clock, and every hour or so a security guard would drive by to check for teenagers making out on the slide or smoking pot in the parking lot.

A silver Honda Civic cruised into the Eden Hope parking lot, shutting off its engine and lights. There was movement in the driver's seat, and the door swung open.

He must have been in his early twenties. His hair, streaked with honeyed-blond highlights, was impeccably styled. Either coming from a party or on his way to one, he wore a crisp white t-shirt, distressed jeans, new sneakers, and a glistening gold watch. A leather backpack hung from one shoulder. He strode toward the largest structure at Eden Hope: the castle.

Many nail-biting parents found the castle dangerous, but it was also the most popular spot in the massive playground. Made of a foggy Plexiglas and weathered by the San Francisco sun and rain for fifteen years, its cramped corridors and stairwells fit children well, but made it difficult for adults to climb in and extract their children.

The man arrived at the castle, checked his watch, then hunched as he entered the arched foyer. He pivoted and traveled a short, narrow staircase, turned again, and continued climbing. Through the semi-transparent walls, he could see that he was now much higher than he would have thought. The castle was just a couple of stories, but when he reached the "top"—a hexagonal room with no proper ceiling and steel supports forming its crest —he could see all of Eden Hope sprawled at his feet.

Only a madman would continue climbing from here.

As he tossed down his backpack, its unbuckled front flap fell open, spilling some of its contents onto the thick, scratched plastic floor. He didn't seem to notice. At about six-and-a-half feet tall, he could reach one hand around the top rim of the wall as no child could. His bicep tensed and flexed as he hauled himself up onto the narrow ledge.

1
A DISTORTED CROWD

"It's such a blessing to be with you fine people tonight," the gregarious Dr. Marcus Demille boomed down into the mic on his podium. Dressed in a beige suit and bright blue tie, he was a looming black man with an immaculately shaved bald head and deep crow's feet. "I've had the distinct pleasure of working with the Charity Medical Center Leukemia Society for almost ten years now, and two years ago, I took the torch from my dear friend, the late Dr. Annabelle Winters …"

As he continued, his baritone easily projecting over the sea of faces seated at the Palace Hotel Restaurant, Marcus lifted his glass in search of one face in particular: Detective Daniel Winters, the late Annabelle's husband. Most of the two or three hundred faces gazed back at him expectantly from their tables, but Dan's face was nowhere in the crowd. He must not have been seated nearby or was not looking up—maybe he didn't even attend—so Marcus cleared his throat, made a passionate toast to Annabelle Winters's brilliance and contribution to science, and ambled into the next section of his speech.

But Detective Winters was there.

Past the hedge of whispered chatter and beyond the buffet laid out toward the back of the hall, slumped a thin, graying figure, studiously examining the label on a bottle of wine. He wore wire-framed reading glasses that often slid down his long, narrow nose. He used to look younger than his age, but since Annie had passed, he felt and looked older. Gray had crept in around his temples and frown lines creased his forehead. Even in one of his finest suits—a gray wool piece on the lapels of which he could still almost feel Annie's touch—he felt old. He didn't know why he had come. He'd told himself he had to.

When he'd arrived an hour earlier, he enjoyed a brief period of serene seclusion before other well-dressed attendees arrived and the merriment ensued. The wine bottle had been sitting in the middle of the table. Shadow Heights Merlot from the Salinas Valley. What was that name supposed to mean? Was it supposed to be sexy, or scary? The label depicted a graying landscape that, like Dan, felt melancholic. The nose had distinct notes of cherry, cranberry, and raspberry, but like the name and the label, the fruit felt drab and tired rather than lively and bright.

Dan had always been sensitive to smells. One of the more memorable experiences from his childhood was when, at the age of five, he had found the source of a Pharaoh ant invasion that had briefly plagued his family home. His little sister had been stashing gummy bears between the sofa cushions, and Dan had sniffed the candy out. This was the tragic end to his sister's secret, and his earliest memory of being highly sensitive to smells.

Then came a brief stint working at a restaurant kitchen, where he had lasted all of two days—the cacophony of odors had been too much for his sixteen-year-old self. The restaurant was a part of an upscale hotel, and Dan had begged his manager to make him a bell-boy. Two years later, he'd transferred back to food and beverages, this time as a bartender. This was his first exposure to the world of wine; his parents had only liked beer.

He still remembered his first whiff of that magic dark-garnet elixir; it had opened his eyes to a whole new universe. Once, a customer had asked for a glass of Torbreck Les Amis, and Dan had expertly uncorked it for him and poured a glass. Immediately, he could smell the jammy blackberry, some cassis, and even possibly a kalamata olive. How could the berry smells go so gloriously with the salty, almost pickled smell of an olive?

He had to know more. Over the next few years, his obsession with wine grew stronger, and by the time he graduated from college, he knew he wasn't going to apply to law schools, as his parents had wanted. Instead, he enrolled in full-time sommelier courses. The rest would have been history, had he not failed his Master exam. He preferred not to think about it too often.

Nosing a wine often pulled Dan into a meditative state—and not just Dan, but anyone who developed an appreciation of wine as more than a beverage with a taste and a smell. Wine, Dan knew, was a carved-out fragment of human life and living nature. Each vintage possesses a distinct signature with its own sense of place and time, the weather that shaped it, the people who poured their sweat into making it, the animals whose diets, life experiences, and decaying bodies fertilized the soil. These aspects of a wine cannot be explained, let alone dissected, but they become part of the hypnotic sensory experience of the liquid in the glass. The enormity of it all invites one to lose oneself in the connections with others who have tasted this unique signature before, creating a more intimate bond between two people who share a bottle than any words can articulate. In this meditative state, Dan often remembered an epic poem from India called *Savitri*. It spoke of a vast, unknown and ever-evolving union that joins all life. Devotees spent years studying the poem to experience this deeply spiritual sense of universal oneness. All Dan required was a single sip of fine wine, properly savored.

The sound of Annie's name startled Dan out of a reverie that had transported him from the restaurant to the Salinas Valley, and then to India. His eyes fluttered and he looked to the front of the hall. The gala, yes. And Demille. Demille had been good to Annie, and Dan would have been happy to support him, but not today. He'd come to show his respect for the foundation to which Annie had dedicated so much of her life, but now that he was here, he just wanted to go home.

It had been two years—not nearly long enough. Being here again, in the same restaurant that the foundation always used, was too much. Everything smelled exactly the same. The vague scents of flame-retardant table linen, overcooked barbecue sauce, and wine. So much wine flowed at these events —you'd think doctors would know better. It worked to loosen purse strings for some, but for others, it only loosened memories.

The wine poured here was often quite average, but Dan had been to enough events at the Palace Hotel to know the bar always had a few gems. Chef Parker Trebor ran the kitchen and was a good friend, one of the few people Dan felt genuinely happy to see. Parker knew Dan wouldn't drink the Shadow Heights swill, so he'd poured him a surprise. Dan nosed the wine and disappeared back into a meditative trance, transported out of the banquet room, but not to the barren landscape where the wine in the glass had been produced. He found himself in a tiny kitchen with a yellow linoleum floor and a plastic cover on the table for two. The colors were bland, and everything looked and smelled aged. Aged like the bottle on the table. It was the Turkey Flat 1985 Barossa Shiraz that he and Annie had shared with friends one evening when they were all young and happily poor in that tiny apartment. The wine had been a gift from Dan's mentor, who had passed, and the vintage was nearing maturity. Even if one might like to keep a cult wine and a piece of a teacher's life forever, one had to let go sometime.

As he tasted his wine now, Dan shed a tear, just like he had back then. He had to let go. The Merlot tonight was young, but the flavors of pepper, roasted meat, and chocolate synapsed somewhere between the nose, the cribriform plate, and the amygdala, causing the memories to resonate and flow. It made the perfect companion to his untouched steak tartar appetizer.

Dan absentmindedly examined the mixed crowd of merrymakers and philanthropists through the dark legs of wine coating his glass. Some of the visitors chuckled together in tight groups, migrating around the room, ignoring Marcus Demille's continued eloquence. Some of them sat ramrod straight and clapped at all the appropriate intervals. Some just enjoyed their meals and drank, like Dan himself was doing.

He cocked his head to the side and stared out at the flurry of faces, doing a double take at the sight of a vaguely familiar man a few tables away … Jack Stevens? The food critic?

Normally, Dan didn't follow the columns of restaurant reviewers, but how could one not love Jack Stevens? The man had a rare acuity of the senses. In his column, "SF Cornucopia," he recognized and shared flawless, irreproachable, yet far from obvious pairings while maintaining a sense of humor and warding away the pretentiousness so typical of the industry. What was more, Dan often agreed with him. Jack's picture always accompanied the articles, so Dan was sure it was Stevens, right in front of him, here at the Palace Hotel Restaurant.

Stevens looked just like his enigmatic photo, older than Dan by a few years, but it was always so hard to tell on charismatic faces prone to smiles. He too wore smart glasses and had trimmed hair going gray. His beard was well groomed, like his hair. He wore a dark blue suit with a black tie, and everything about his demeanor said he was not here for the fundraiser. He was enjoying his tartare, pink enough that you could see the blood from a few feet away.

But then again, it might not have been Stevens, and Dan settled back, thinking indifferently, *Why does it matter anyway?* His mind shifted to Chef Parker. He had made friends with the young, eccentric chef many years earlier when attending endless and irrelevant galas with Annie, and he knew the man was passionate, committed, and would rise to run the restaurant before long. Dan was also certain that this rise meant his friend spent a portion of his time being lonely, overworked, and underappreciated.

If that really was Stevens, then Parker was being visited by an incisive food critic, and the chef would have known as soon as Stevens stepped through the door. Maybe Parker would appreciate some friendly comfort.

Up at the front of the large hall, Marcus's shining scalp moved about as if punctuating the passion in his words. Dan rose to his feet, and as soon as he did, that voice boomed into the mic, "There's the man I've been looking for. Ladies and gentlemen, this is the late Dr. Annabelle Winters's husband, Detective Daniel Winters. Thank you so much for coming out, sir. We greatly appreciate your continued efforts for our cause. Let's give him a hand!"

For one horrible, excruciating moment, all the attention was on Dan. Every face swung to beam up at him, all the hands were slapping together in his honor, and he suddenly couldn't remember how to smile. The best he could do was swallow and nod. He almost raised one limp hand in a gesture of defense.

Perhaps Marcus recognized the seasick expression on Dan's face, because he redirected his rhetoric and added, "And thank you all so much for coming out tonight. Give yourselves a round of applause!"

Thank God.

All those grinning faces turned at last, freeing Dan from their grip. He strode away, quicker than necessary, toward the swinging kitchen doors so near to his table. As a waiter holding a tray of summer salads stepped past, Dan's attention returned to reality and his senses came to a focus. There were cut strawberries (on the verge of turning bad, and at their sweetest) and roasted sunflower seeds in a thin base of red wine vinegar over fragrant shallots—and then it was gone, the ambient noise came back, and Dan passed into the commotion beyond.

Deep, piping-hot tubs of soup sat on stoves, burbling, and pans scintillated with strips of chicken and steak. The assault on Dan's nostrils was complete and harrowing, reminding his of those brief two days when he tried working in a restaurant kitchen. His eyes watered from the intensity of the experience as cooks hurtled past him, searching for this or that. Dan wove as gracefully and efficiently as he could through this madness, until he finally located a fluffy white chef's hat.

"Parker," he called.

Parker Trebor was Scottish to the core, with deeply freckled arms and, beneath the chef's hat, a jungle of thick red curls. He was only in his late twenties, too young to be the master of such a prestigious kitchen, Dan guessed, as his friend's generous belly defied gravity through frantic stirring, and the chef blossomed with notes of stress, sweat, and inexpensive cologne.

As Parker turned, Dan smelled the subtle yet unmistakable odor of adrenaline, also known as fear. Betrayed by bloodshot, glassy eyes and dry, colorless lips, his friend was visibly freaking out. Parker frowned at the sight of Dan, as if any other man could only be here to slow him down.

"Is that Jack Stevens out there?" Dan asked.

"Sure as heck is," Parker said, his voice seesawing from one octave to the next. He turned away hurriedly and continued adding spices to his sauce. "He asked for my recommendation, and I recommended the sweet salmon for the first course. I … I don't know. I don't know. It looked good going out just now. What did you think? Did it look bad? Did it smell bad? Fuck, it smelled bad."

Dan had to smile at this kid. He cared so much. It must feel good to care so deeply about something.

"I wish I could give you some advice, but my forte is wine, not so much food. Would you like me to recommend a pairing for you, though?"

Parker's face tightened into a scowl. "Ha. Because you used to be a somm?" His tone was acidic. "I know about wines too, you know."

Passionate, devoted, and hypersensitive.

Parker snatched up a cold, crusty pan from nearby and shoved it under Dan's nose. "This was the salmon I made him. Give it your best shot."

Dan took a deep breath through his nose, letting it all wash over him. The cloying sweetness was the most striking feature of the fish. The red glaze had been raspberries. Honey also played no small role. Of course, salmon was a sweet fish, juicy and succulent all on its own, the luscious creaminess further thickened by a dusting of cinnamon and clove.

Parker clearly had a wine in mind and merely sought agreement. "I think a New World Chardonnay would be predict—I mean, safe pairing. Is that what you were thinking?" Dan said. Parker nodded, just slightly. "But I smell pink, Parker."

"Pink? Because the fish is pink? That's not how you pair, detective!"

Parker clearly didn't connect, so Dan explained. "A Rosé. You need bright just-ripe berries that jump out of the glass with the sweetness of the salmon. The acid of the wine will dissolve the fat and sugar away. You won't even have to redo your salmon."

He knew the kid was walking a tightrope right now. Blowing off some steam at Dan was just helping him focus. "That's just what I'm thinking," Dan said.

"All right, but you're crowding me," Parker said roughly. "Get out of here, let me think."

Dan shrugged and complimented him on the steak all the same, then ducked through the back door to avoid the crowd of philanthropists on the other side of the kitchen.

"Wait!" Parker said. "Which one from our menu? We just have three."

"None of those." Dan paused as he allowed Parker to fume a moment. "When I visited your place across the street, you had a Chapel Down English Rosé from Kent that you brought back from seeing your mom."

Parker smirked. "Very funny, Dan—really, bravo. That's the cheap stuff she buys at a local market. I only brought it back because she made me."

"Have one of your guys run across the street to get it—you won't regret it. Stevens will destroy any Chardonnay you put in front of him."

The young man looked momentarily flabbergasted at the idea of following this mad recommendation before he settled back into the frantic pace that had become his baseline. Dan shrugged again, then turned and strode out the door.

❀

Five days later, Dan stood in another kitchen, washing his hands before he touched anything. This one wasn't filled with the same terror and stress that money creates for one of the most enjoyable activities humans have. This kind of cooking filled Dan with the sense of peace and homecoming that was now almost entirely absent from his daily life. A happy home has an aroma, one of the hardest to describe. Just as *umami* is a perception of taste, Dan often thought of *hygge* as a smell that combines all the right olfactory signals to feel at home and at ease. The Porters' home had that smell.

"What are you meditating over while being in my way?" A caring female voice brought him back to Earth, and Dan flinched slightly as a gentle pair of hands braced his sides and edged him over a foot or two.

Rachel Porter filled the space Dan had just been occupying, busily washing her own hands as well. A petite brunette, she had her straight hair clasped loosely at the base of her neck in a wood-grain clip. She wore a pale-blue cardigan, khakis, and pearl necklace, earrings, and bracelets, contrasting sharply with Dan's slate-colored palette and sun-kissed complexion. The scent of lime and sea salt tided to Dan: all-natural cleansing agents. Pleasant enough, but the smell of raw chicken on the cutting board wasn't easily overcome.

Another voice floated in from behind them, this one deep and fatherly. "Sorry I'm late." Boris was a physician and an old friend to both Dan and Annie. Rachel's husband appeared much older than his forties, with a ruddy complexion and a thick beard. He had begun losing his youthful shape a few years before and cooking fresh dinners had become the nightly tradition to stave off what he called "the inevitable." Dan and Annie had come to the first such dinner three or four years ago, and through his subsequent ordeals, the Friday night tradition remained one of the few that Dan had kept. It may well have saved him. It wasn't so much the food as the silent love, acceptance, and patience given by others that helped and healed, instead of those who superficially asked, "Dan, are you okay? You know you can always talk to me."

He remembered how he'd had that same feeling with Annie, as though nothing more was required or necessary apart from just being. Whenever he stepped out of the enveloping aroma of safety, Dan felt as if the insatiable world demanded something from him, pulled at him, and ripped him apart. He was grateful to Annie for that. And grateful to Boris and Rachel, for reminding him of what life should be like.

"I was trying to sneak out the ER entrance," Boris went on, his beard sweeping a kiss over Rachel's blushed cheek. Only the best of friends would appreciate the forceful punch to Dan's shoulder that followed. "But there was a bus crash of homicidal pregnant patients with salmonella, and well, nobody does that better than I. Nothing makes me want to cook chicken more than salmonellosis. Honey, scalpel," he winked at Rachel while reaching for the chef's knife.

"I think you're forgetting that at home, you're not in charge. Plus, you are tardy," Rachel said with a straight face, striking the spatula on the counter hard enough to make a snapping sound and pushing her husband against the countertop. "Dan, cuff him. And read him his rights."

Rachel really was in charge today, but Boris was not to be sidelined. Though he didn't have rights to the chicken, he turned on his personal art in the kitchen, the art of the *amuse-bouche*. He was able to combine ingredients into the most ingenious bite-sized pieces, and to his wife's delight spoiled her and Dan with a never-the-same whirlwind tour of world cuisine in a single bite. He was his usual creative self.

Rachel scooped up the slippery slabs of chicken, dumping them into the prepared bowl of golden marinade: fresh orange pulp, the palpable saltiness of soy sauce, a splash of lemon, and a crust of panko breadcrumbs and brown sugar. The ingredients danced in an olfactory state of balance that made it seem they could never be apart. As always, this was going to be good. Damn, I wish Annie were here, Dan thought. And damn, it was Annie who taught Rachel this recipe. Grief came back when he least expected it, yet his friends, whether or not they knew what he was thinking, pretended to carry on and lead Dan out of the holes he stepped in as he struggled to shake off despair.

This time as well, Rachel continued tossing sliced multicolored peppers resembling Olympic rings into a fragrant fish stock, and Boris set the table. Dan started to feel better.

"Last Saturday," Rachel said, glancing at Dan, "how'd the gala go?" She handed Boris the dishes.

"Oh, it was horrible as always." Dan made his tone more frivolous than was necessary. Boris grabbed a big handful of emerald-green beans and dumped them into a cold pot on the stove. Dan spoke brightly. "I don't remember ever having been applauded before, so this one was especially grim. 'Let's all applaud for your loss, Dan,'" he said sarcastically. As soon as the words left his lips, he lowered his eyes, cursing to himself. He hadn't meant to sound so bitter.

It had only been two years. Not even two, yet. He counted the days as they bled onward. Counted the seasons. Nothing went unmarked in respect to Annie's death. It was how he told time now. His mind was elsewhere. Damn it. He hoped Rachel and Boris hadn't noticed.

But they had.

"I'm sorry, Dan," Rachel whispered. "I—" Her mouth folded in at the corners, and her eyes blinked hard, as if she were uncertain about her next words. "I always thought you went back to work too soon. Maybe—"

"Work keeps my head on," Dan reminded her, forcing a light smile. "It's just a road I must travel. I'm fine."

Boris exhaled and picked up Dan's tenor, slapping him on the shoulder and returning to dousing the green beans in salt, oil, and a light squeeze of lemon juice. "He's right, Rach," Boris said. "Work is good for a man. Otherwise, he'd move in with us. Imagine watching Danish drama on TV every day. I would never be able to have white Zin again."

Rachel rolled her eyes and stirred the rice.

Dan went to grease the pan for the orange chicken, but as his hands moved, so did his mind. He didn't know—how much mourning was normal? Hadn't it been long enough? Should he ask Boris? He had never known another person who'd lost their spouse suddenly, at a young age, and from leukemia. He could ask his parents for advice, but their marriage had been brief and bitter.

Just as the butter layer coated the bottom of the long pan, a vibration from his right pocket called him away from his thoughts. His hand extracted the device, which read, "Chief," as it did often, but it never failed to dent Dan's mouth on one side.

"Chief" was Chief Lester Brigham, who had been a mountainous fixture at the San Francisco Police Department since long before Dan's time. Years back, he was a tall, good-looking detective, but now his hair was ash white and as thin as stubble, his face's folds looked like a pug's expression, and his mouth was set resolutely to never yield a smile unless it was at one of his own jokes. He never seemed to care much for anybody, and Dan did his part by trying to treat him with respect.

It was as though Chief had heard that Dan needed work to distract him. He swiped over the green phone icon and brought it to his ear. Leaving the kitchen, he slid through an open glass door leading out onto the porch, where he was blinded by sun-splashed foliage clustered in pots and freely growing in the yard. That wasn't the only sense temporarily dazzled; it was mid-August in California, and his nostrils flooded with the pungent but pleasant smell of cut grass, quickly followed by another, more distant odor—the chemical smell of lighter fluid and charcoal, making a comeback now that the novelty of natural gas had worn off.

Dan grimaced and turned his eyes to the cherrywood boards beneath his feet. That was easier, as the weathered wood had its own ripe aroma.

"Chief," he said politely.

"What are you doing?"

"I was just about to have dinner with friends," Dan answered. "But I can cut it short."

"I think you should. A young female's body was discovered in Excelsior. She's been dead for a week. The neighbors just noticed the smell. She had her AC cranked to high heaven. You'd better meet me there."

2
THE NAGGING NOTE

Dan sighed and turned to the bright window not far from the Porter family porch, where he could see Boris and Rachel rushing around, scooping rice onto plates. Despite the obvious mood of hurry, they were smiling, and he heard Rachel shriek as Boris dodged her with a plate piled with hot green beans. The chicken must be close to finished. His mouth filled with saliva ... but he would have to wait.

He briefly considered grabbing some greasy fast food on the way, but quickly discarded the idea. His sensitive palate wouldn't allow him to do certain things to himself.

By the time Dan arrived at the scene, Unit #36 of Bay View Apartments, the dazzling sunset had deepened to a rich navy blue. The door hung wide open, and there was a stretcher going out as he entered, cloaked in the thick darkness of a body bag. His eyes tracked it as he sidestepped the medics —"Hey Charley, Merv," he said—and watched it go by in slow motion, a sick roll in his stomach. Although he had no regret over being in this line of work, some days could be hard. He was surprised by the sheer number of promising people who ended their lives prematurely in this city.

When Dan stepped into the studio apartment, the overwhelming odor of fresh paint assaulted him—the walls were a cheerful, pale yellow, almost watery, striped with a tonal lime—and the smell was at odds with the incredible sour of decay. The combination was abominable, and Dan pressed the back of his palm to his nostrils to muffle it.

"There's our Magic Man," Chief Lester called out when he saw Dan. He was crouched in the center of the den, examining a stack of neon leaflets on the tabletop. Two other officers—Barry North, nicknamed "North Star" by the Chief, and Juan Manozza, whom Chief had dubbed "the Man"—were present in the room, taking notes and ambling around. Barry was a slim Canadian, blue-eyed, black-haired, and fair-skinned, in his early twenties. He often had a dazed look when he saw blood. A pretty boy. Probably wouldn't stay with the force much longer. Juan was older, from Arizona, with muscles stacked on top of each other by grueling gym sessions. He had tattooed hands, hair thicker than Jesus's, and an extreme coffee addiction. Dan could always smell the rich acidity of the beans on him. He was holding a sealed plastic bag just now, probably containing the weapon the victim had used.

Chief called Dan Magic Man because he seemed to pull answers from "up his sleeve" (or, from time to time, a more verbally colorful section of the anatomy). But the chief knew that no answers came from Dan's sleeve; they were all stashed up his nose.

"Sorry, I'm late." Dan answered Chief in a nasal voice, as he refused to use his nostrils for breathing right now. It was just too much. The neighbors might not have smelled poor Amanda's rot for a week, but if Dan had lived upstairs, he would have known the very next day. It permeated everything in the apartment. Original scents remained, but only under a thick residue of death and fresh paint. "I took a bus."

Chief cracked a smile and shoved a thumb toward Dan, rolling his eyes. "This guy," he said shaking his head.

Dan tilted his head back and forth. "It saves gas."

"You save my ass," Chief countered.

Dan opened his mouth, but no words emerged. There was no comeback for that.

"Since you missed the girl, I'll catch you up." Chief pushed himself to a slow stand on his deteriorating knees. Chief Lester had always possessed a barrel of a chest, but as he aged (and filled his body with cheap, addictive garbage), his waist had expanded to catch up with it. Now his entire torso was a bulging barrel, and Dan could only imagine what would happen if the old man was forced to take the stairs. "Amanda Turner was a Caucasian female, twenty-eight years of age," he said. "She was discovered a few hours ago, when the building manager responded to complaints of a strong odor. She hanged herself from a very stable support beam."

Dan's eyes moved around the apartment as Chief spoke. The decor of any room spoke volumes about its owner, and this was no different. There was clutter on the floor: flip-flops, a hairbrush, ripped jeans.

"Did she have any roommates?" Officer Barry asked.

"She sure did," Chief said with a caustic edge to his voice. "That's why it took a whole week to find her body, North Star. Because she had so many roommates coming in and out."

Barry cleared his throat, looking sheepish. "Right," he said.

Posters on the walls portrayed famed musicians across all genres throughout modern times, from Janis Joplin to Jay-Z, Cher to … "Who's the guy with a half-shaved head?" Dan said.

"Damned if I know," Chief muttered.

"Uh, Skrillex," Juan answered, though he was the second oldest male in the room after Chief. It should have been Barry, who was still young enough to follow pop music. "He does, well—it's electronic-type stuff."

Chief crinkled his mouth with disapproval but nodded. "Looks like she was working as a deejay at that club, Episodes," he said, flipping the orange leaflets in his hand back onto the coffee table. The only other surfaces in the room were two bookshelves and one small table alongside a worn brown couch. Dan saw one framed picture on a side table: a young, brunette woman giving a sideways peace sign, wearing aviator shades perched on top of her head, enough makeup to completely change the shape and features of a human face, and gobs of chestnut curls cascading over her shoulders. Beneath the metric ton of foundation, Amanda had been very pretty. Dan could only imagine what the corpse in the body bag now looked like.

In the picture, a young black man stood next to Amanda, his arm around her shoulders. He had bleached dreadlocks and a septum piercing. They were on a pier, and they looked happy.

"Went by the name of LA Deej, which is funny 'cause she's not from LA," Chief was going on from over Dan's shoulder. "Into music. Into fashion. Into drugs."

Dan approached the bookshelf next, still holding the framed pier picture in his hand.

The bookshelf was cluttered with delicate glass vases and bowls, inside of which were withered honeysuckle flowers and dried peach slices. Dan ran his fingers through them absently, then ducked to examine the actual books on the shelf. He could see why Chief thought Amanda was into music, fashion, and drugs. The books were mostly dedicated to makeup techniques, hair care, music history, and how to tend various strains of marijuana. Two books didn't fit with the others, though: language guides to Italian and Slovenian. Had Amanda been planning a trip?

"Hmm," Dan murmured. He didn't mean to sound doubtful, but he felt as if there might be more here than met the eye. "If she was going to kill herself, why would she paint the walls?"

Chief glowered at Dan. He was always asking questions like this, and it always earned the cranky man's ire.

"It doesn't look fresh to me," Chief grumbled. "Why do you think it's fresh?"

"Wait—I smell it too," Barry said. "I couldn't place it—I thought it was just the body odor, but he's right. It's paint. You can barely smell it."

"Huh," Chief said. "I guess smoking all those years ago must've singed all my nose hairs."

"That does add a new element to the case," Juan said.

But Chief grimaced still. "I don't think it's enough to start talking about murder," he replied in that snide tone he often used with Dan's theories. "Typical suicides are going to have substance-abuse histories and lack of support network. We've got her living alone. We've got her drug history. We don't know if there was abuse, but it looks like she had a boyfriend. Probably another partier like her."

Chief nodded toward the frame in Dan's hand, and Dan reacted by popping open the back and extracting the picture. Written in a bubbly female print were the words, "Me and Jermaine, summer '16."

"They look happy to me," Dan said.

"Yeah? Well, they weren't," Chief snapped back at him. His nostrils flared. "Same neighbors who reported the smell also told us that Amanda was in a lot of loud arguments a few weeks ago—with a male. So, we've got the drugs. We've got the loneliness. We've got the possible breakup. We've got the rope. I see *fait accompli* scrawled all over this, boys."

Dan didn't buy it, but there wasn't enough confounding data present to change Chief's mind—not the boy in the picture or the fresh paint on the walls. Dan knew better than to mention the language guides, which could have been purchased for any college class five years before. Still, it nagged at him. Why would a suicidal woman paint her apartment? He needed more.

"I'll be right back." Dan excused himself, stepping back out into the hall. He reached into the pocket of his suit jacket, where dense, smooth plastic crinkled at his touch. He extracted a rolled-up bag of Ethiopian Harrar coffee beans, opening it beneath his nose. He breathed in the strong scent, washing away the competitive odors of decay and paint, then stepped back into the room.

New notes arose from the air, and he tucked the dense plastic pouch back into his suit pocket.

"What you doin' out there, Magic Man?" Chief cocked his head slightly at Dan. "Meditating on coffee beans?"

Dan dragged a deep, careful pull through his nose and savored the variety of messages that filtered through his sophisticated olfactory palate. Now he could smell the peaches and honeysuckle. And … and ham?

He frowned and followed the peculiar sweet, dry note of cured meat, leading him to several thin shreds of crumpled, darkened prosciutto in the carpet fibers. Amid all the clutter, it was easy to miss, but when you could smell it, you could find it.

He plucked a ribbon of dried meat from the floor and presented it to Chief Lester. "What about this?" he said, skirting the meat beneath his own nose for a deeper pull. "Prosciutto di san Daniele left out on the floor?"

"Prosh-what-dee-who?" Chief barked back at him.

"Prosciutto—it's an Italian ham."

"I know what prosciutto is," Chief snapped. "What was that other stuff about?"

"This prosciutto is from a particular region, and it's very fine. It's rare. Artisanal. Expensive. You wouldn't —uh—leave it on your carpet. Not unless there was something you were trying to—"

"You might if you were losing it," Chief interrupted with a shrug. "I still don't see murder just because you found ham. You know what I'm looking at, while you're looking at that old picture and some coffee beans? I'm looking at this." The frustrated chief nodded to Juan, who was standing idle by the front door now. "Show him that rope, my man."

Juan held out a clear plastic bag, sealed. Dan took it and, without opening it, examined the length of rope knotted into a noose.

"You see that?" Chief asked, ambling over to them. "It's damn intricate, ain't it?"

Dan frowned and held the rope closer to his eyes. It wasn't just intricate, it was beautiful. Handwoven. The rope wasn't frayed and haggard like most rope; the texture was silky, even through the plastic, and the cords were emerald and gold. The threads traveled horizontally. The grain of most rope ran vertical, but this—it reminded him of something. He had seen it somewhere before.

"Handwoven," Chief said, voicing Dan's thoughts. "Handwoven, Magic Man. Maybe she painted the damn walls because she's detail oriented, and she wanted to go out in a yellow room, you know? Wanted to go out in a yellow and green room with a yellow and green rope. Sounds like a psychotic break if I ever heard one, you know? How long do you think weaving this took?"

"I—don't know," Dan admitted. "At least a day. My wife and I saw basket weavers when we were on our honeymoon in Italy. They were out in the streets from dawn to dusk."

"Exactly," Chief agreed, suddenly hearty. He must have known he'd won. "This girl spent time weaving her own hanging rope. She wanted to die. I can't tell you why. Probably had something to do with breaking up with that boy. But I can tell you it didn't have a thing to do with some old ham on the floor, and he didn't murder her."

Dan relented.

On his way home on the bus, his cell phone vibrated. Boris's picture flashed on the screen, with his cheesy grin, sweating profusely in a Hawaiian shirt, toasting with a mixed drink. Dan was grateful to swipe his finger and bring the phone to his ear. After dealing with Chief, he needed a different kind of palate cleanser. Bosses were difficult—and bosses who had no faith in him, doubly so.

"Hey, Boris." Dan heard the exhaustion seeping from his voice despite his effort to be lighthearted. "How's it going? Sorry to skip out on dinner like that."

"Oh, it's all right," Boris replied, sounding hearty. He was probably full to the brim, having eaten both his own and Dan's portions, though Rachel rarely let him get away with that kind of stuff. "We were sad to see you go. Can we give it another try?"

In the background, Dan could discern Rachel's hushed whisper to Boris, something about how Dan needed to talk. And "get it out"? Maybe he should have been offended that they would whisper about him right in front of him (or his phone, in this case), but he was only amused. It was nice to have friends who cared enough about him to whisper about his well-being.

"I would love that," Dan replied. "Tomorrow eve-ning? How would that suit you?"

"Perfect," Boris answered brightly. "You pick the meal, we all cook, we all eat."

"Mmm. Hmm. I don't know. Oh, wait. You know what? I have a curious craving for antipasto. What do you think of that?"

"Eh, it's a little light for a dinner, isn't it?"

"Then let me make it. It won't seem light anymore."

Boris laughed. "All right, all right, you win."

Dan brightened. He got to win so rarely anymore. "I don't know what it is," he added. "I have the most curious craving for a big dish of antipasto, and a nice, cold glass of Friulano."

Dan began his morning doing the standard yoga poses, things Annie had taught him that were now impossible to forget. Flowing through the asanas, still wearing his boxer briefs, he felt closer to her somehow. Almost as if she were there. Before she became so sick, they had risen with the sun and performed the downward dog and warrior poses together in their underwear, or whatever it was they had slept in. From time to time, he'd been lucky enough to see Annie doing yoga in a special negligée—or nothing at all. When she tucked her chin during the child's pose, her long, silver-and-gold hair tumbled over her trim, muscled shoulders like a waterfall.

He tried very hard to not think of Annie's body. He was okay with remembering moments with her. That was inescapable. But he never let himself imagine her, fantasize about her, the way he had when she was flesh and blood and—

Dan blinked, casting the images from his mind, and went from child's pose to the cat-cow flow. Breathe, he reminded himself, intentionally deleting the memory of Annie's hair. This was about relaxation, not stress. He tried to clear his mind, but thoughts invaded. Why would Amanda Turner spend all that time painting her room, and weaving the rope? And how could they be sure she'd woven it? What were the fights with the boyfriend about? What if there was no breakup to blame? He hadn't even seen—or more aptly, smelled—the body, only the week-old stench it had left behind.

His eyes snapped open. He'd gotten into tree pose and completely forgotten to focus on his breath because he'd been thinking about women. Dead women.

I need to be sure, he thought. If not for myself, for Jermaine or whoever else might need the closure of knowing Amanda hadn't chosen to leave that way. It would be a disservice to them to not make absolutely certain it had been suicide.

Dan nodded to himself, resolute now. He'd forgotten to focus on his breathing again, but at least he had made up his mind about how he was going to spend his Saturday: at the morgue.

Denise was normally the morgue worker on Saturdays and Sundays, but it looked as though the schedule had changed. Vincent Ciccia, an irreverent twerp barely out of the pre-med program, usually worked Mondays to Wednesdays, but here he was on a Saturday afternoon. Vincent, a man with his head so far up his own ass Dan didn't know how his earbuds reached their phone jack. Dan didn't normally think such coarse thoughts about other human beings, but Vinnie showed no respect for death. He didn't fear it like he should.

He hadn't seen it happen yet.

Just now, he was idly examining the wall of slabs, his kinky auburn hair past his ears, two white head-phone cords dangling like earrings.

Dan didn't look at him. He was trying to smell the aged corpse of Amanda Turner for any notes that might be counterintuitive to suicide.

Something was there, an undercurrent. So light, so elusive, even his nose couldn't quite identify it. Almost like … an oak tree? Wood? A nut? He could not place the scent any further than that. He had no choice but to thank Vinnie and let him get back to his anatomy homework in peace.

It looked like Chief had won. Maybe Dan was wrong after all.

He filled his plate eagerly from the larger platter of traditional meats, cheeses, olives, peppers, mushrooms, and artichoke hearts. The spread was cold and oily, and sprinkled with spices. Dan loved it.

"What was that wine you said to pair with this?" Boris asked as he plucked an artichoke heart from his plate and shoved it into his mouth.

Dan couldn't help but grin. "Friulano, if you have it." The Porters's wine selection had improved dramatically since befriending Dan and Annie—two wine lovers to the core—but it was far from perfect.

"I think we do," Rachel said to Boris as he retreated to the next room to scour their rack. "So, Dan." She folded her arms in front of herself on the table. Her eyes were intense and solemn, which was unusual for her, and she cast them in Boris's direction, as if trying to convey something before he got back. Her voice hushed another notch. "I wanted to talk to you about something you said the other night."

"Son of a gun, we do have it," Boris boomed.

Rachel looked away from Dan, distracted by her husband's triumphant return. Boris popped the cork, pouring the ethereal yellow into Dan's empty glass. Dan was relieved that Boris's unwitting assistance had helped him avoid an "important conversation." Right now, he just wanted to eat this delicious meal and savor the wine that went with it.

As Boris poured the Friulano into Rachel's glass, Dan forked a delicate portion of prosciutto di san Daniele into his mouth. Mmm. The salty, smoky slivers melted on his tongue, and he took a quick sniff of the Friulano as he brought his glass to his nose.

His nostrils flared, and he paused. That nagging note … the woodsy, nutty scent, flat and earthy … could it have been almonds, the same tiny note that tided to him now, in this glass?

"Dan." Boris's voice invaded his epiphany. "You were saying?"

Dan's eyes darted up from the bright yellow liquid in his glass. "I wasn't saying anything."

"About this new case," Boris reminded him, taking his seat after filling his own glass. "About how Lester wouldn't listen again, even though he must call you Magic Man for a reason, you would think. He must ac-knowledge that your methods, however inexplicable to him, are valuable."

"Maybe," Dan said, but his mind was leagues away as he added absently, "I went to the morgue and smelled her."

The two of them flinched. Of course, they knew about his olfactory abilities, but this—Rachel's eyes flashed with horror, and Dan wondered briefly if he was on the edge of losing it and didn't know it.

He swallowed and forced himself to go on. "And I did smell something I couldn't quite place, certainly not in the typical bouquet of decay."

"Bouquet of decay," Boris parroted. "I think we've finally got the name of our metal band, Dan."

"It was bitter and wooden, flat—earthy," he went on, ignoring Boris's attempt at a joke. "Like almonds. Bad almonds."

Rachel grinned. "Ooh, The Bad Almonds, another good band name—"

"Wait, honey," Boris interrupted with a raised finger. "Bitter almonds, Dan?"

Dan shrugged. "I think so."

"Bitter almond is the scent of cyanide. I mean, I'm not saying you have something, but I'd recommend forensics take another look before she goes in the ground."

Dan felt a steely hand grip his guts at Boris's words. Had he done it? Was he right?

He took a tentative sip of his Friulano, hoping he wasn't. Being wrong would make everything so much easier.

Of all the pathologists at the SFPD crime lab, the girlish Eunice Boddington was Dan's favorite. Well, she wasn't a girl—she was probably in her early fifties—but she conducted herself as if she was no older than seventeen. Dan didn't know how she managed it. Eunice had dark-chocolate eyes that glowed with awe, cinnamon-colored hair constantly styled in the old Farrah look, and the smooth, clear skin of a teenager. Although she had the body of a grown woman, she wore flirty, vibrant dresses as successfully as if she were still the svelte and dewy gal she must have been on that old disco floor. Her makeup was impeccable, not that Dan was any sort of expert.

Dan's spirits always lifted when Eunice was the pathologist on the clock. She made him feel special. Her smile was always so ready and warm that he figured she would give him anything he wanted. But when he mentioned bringing Amanda Turner back from the morgue, she set a firm boundary: "That's a bad idea, Dan."

"I know the body's down there," Dan said, a flush creeping up his neck.

"I've already seen her from head to toe. That examination took me almost three hours. In suspected suicides, I'm always extra thorough." Her pitch seemed to come almost out of the top of her head, it was so pinched and pressurized. He wasn't used to bickering with her. She had already said no. She'd been the examiner for that report, and she was sticking by it. Simple cause of death: suicide by strangulation. "As much as I hate how dismissive it sounds to say, 'open and shut,'" she said, "in this case, it's apt."

Clearly, she didn't get why this was important. For that matter, neither did Dan. But for whatever reason, it was important to him, so he persisted.

As Eunice listened, she tilted her head, considering. Then she exhaled in a huff. "Did you know this Amanda woman, Dan? Be honest. She was maybe some girl you babysat? Old friend's daughter? What?"

"No," Dan insisted. "It's not personal." Or was it? He put the thought out of his mind. "It's nothing like that. I had never seen her before going down to the morgue. Not even at the scene."

Eunice frowned. "You went and looked at her in the morgue," she confirmed. "By yourself. And you found ... something noteworthy, I guess?"

"I don't know," he said, bluffing. "I can't explain it to you. Call it a hunch. Hell, call it a favor, Eunice."

She leaned back on her heels and slanted her mouth to one side. Dan could see her shoulders relax, the fight draining out of her, and knew she'd been vanquished. "You've never come in here before, asking to get a body exhumed."

"I'm hoping it doesn't come to that."

"Don't be smart. You know what I mean." She sighed dramatically and her eyelashes kissed shut. She let her head roll back on her neck and groaned, "Okay. Okay. Normally, I wouldn't. But for you, Detective Winters—this once—I will look again."

She opened her eyes and righted her head. Dan smiled. She was still shaking her head at him as she walked back through the automatic sliding glass doors to the crime lab, but she was going to do it, nonetheless.

For the rest of the day and evening, Dan put the mystery of Amanda Turner's handwoven rope to the back of his mind. His sleep was fitful and brief, and he awoke to find the morning sticky and unforgiving. He felt old. Glaring at the empty side of his bed, he swung his feet to the floor and thumped, like a zombie, to the bathroom. After a long, hot shower, he dressed in a suit, even though it was in the upper nineties outside, and he wasn't required to. Annie had loved a man in a suit, so it had become his habit. He couldn't picture himself any other way anymore.

A cup of coffee and a bus ride later, Dan was in the hall at work, striding past the crime lab, when he heard the sliding glass doors open behind him and a voice calling his name. It was Eunice, in a thin orange dress under her lab coat, jogging toward him in four-inch heels. What an amazing piece of work, he thought with pure admiration. Not for her looks, specifically—for her.

"Dan!" Eunice called breathlessly. "How did you know?" Her feet might have been used to walking around on stilts, but her lungs weren't accustomed to running in any footwear. She held her side and gasped for breath, shooting him an occasional watery smile as if to reassure him that she wasn't about to keel over. "Out with it, hot stuff. What was that hunch you had?"

Dan tilted his head to one side and said, almost flirting, "Tell me what you found, and I'll tell you what I know."

"You dog." Eunice grinned and pushed into him tiredly. He didn't think he'd ever seen her with a hair out of place until now, but she didn't seem to mind. "There was something we missed after all. I almost didn't see it this time, either, but there was definitely a needle injection site on a vein in the big toe. Thirty gauge, tiny. We're running a toxicology on her right now." She beamed up at Dan, her dimples showing. "Good job, kid."

He was forty-two, but he let it slide. "Thanks, Eunice."

At his desk, Dan logged onto Facebook and looked up the name Amanda Turner, cross-referenced with San Francisco. At first, she didn't pop up—until he typed in "LA Deej." A thumbnail picture of a girl in a black vinyl corset appeared on the screen. This picture was clearly taken for publicity purposes; she was wearing some kind of ballgown that looked like it was made from a trash bag. Her lipstick was matte black, and her lip was pierced. He clicked on the link, and it opened to her public page.

Her most recent entry was almost a month old, and it read: "Moving on, San Fran scene. Say *bonjour* to Amanda Leroy."

Amanda Leroy? Who's that? Could Leroy be the last name of her new significant other? A Frenchman?

Dan clicked on her timeline and saw that she was with a Jermaine Beal (who also had a Facebook account) from 2014 to the current year. He clicked on Jermaine's profile and took note of the phone number listed in the biography, entering it into his cell phone immediately and hitting send.

It rang almost eight times before a male voice picked up. "Hello?" He sounded preoccupied, like he'd moved on to something else already rather than wasting time on grief.

"Hello. Is this Jermaine Beal?"

"Speaking. Who's this?"

"My name is Detective Daniel Winters, and I'm with the San Francisco Police Department."

A hush fell across the line. Then: "Oh, shit."

"What's wrong?"

"I guess this is probably about Amanda."

"Yes, it is. Can you answer some questions for me right now?"

There was a hesitation. "I guess. I got nothin' to hide."

"What was your relationship with her?"

"Um … that's complicated. We met at Episodes, worked together for a while there. I was the bouncer, she was the deejay. Uh, things were going really good. And then, a few weeks, maybe a few months ago, she starts changing. I don't know. I let it go. Shit happens."

Dan sat up straighter in his chair. "She started changing?"

"Yeah. Changing. She starts to get pretentious as shit. Doesn't want to be a deejay anymore. Doesn't want to smoke anymore. Doesn't want to go out anymore. I said fine. I'll come over. She says she don't want me to come over. So, we're fighting. She's pushing me away, she's done with me. There's someone else. So, I left."

"Did she say there was someone else?"

"Didn't have to. People don't just change their whole selves like that for no reason."

"Did you ever see her again, after that last fight?"

"Nope. I freelance. I'm working as a bodyguard right now; it's a 24/7 job. The gig's in Los Angeles, and it's not set to wrap until fall. So, I figured, you know, that's plenty of time to get away from her, get my space, forget about it."

"You've been in LA for how long?"

"Mm. Three weeks and change."

"And you've been there every day since."

"Yep. Don't have time to travel right now. I live in this guy's backyard. I literally live in his yard, watching his house all damn night. Got a trailer hitched to my truck, man. Come on out and see for yourself."

"Did Amanda ever mention the name of this other person? Did she mention any new names?"

"Not to me. I don't know. You might want to check with some of her other friends—people who were into her scene, because she ran in some different circles than me. This guy, the one who changed her, he didn't come from my scene. But she had other friends, family connections, shit from her past. You might want to check with some of these cats—like Branden. Uh, shit, I can't remember the other names."

"I'm going to need a little more to go on than the name Branden, Mr. Beal," Dan said warmly. He didn't want to offend the guy.

"Uh, yeah, I'm not sure of the other names. She never really hung out with me and them at the same time. Different lifestyles. Branden Bull-something?"

Dan sighed. It had almost been a lead, for a second. "Thanks anyway, sir. I appreciate your time."

"Look, I heard she killed herself. It's all over, every-body knows, but—I don't know, man. She was mad at me when I left, but she wasn't suicidal. I've never thought of Amanda as suicidal. She was a happy woman. No, not happy. But stable. I can say that."

"Did you see the Facebook post she made last month, in which she told her followers to say *'bonjour'* to 'Amanda Leroy'?"

"Yeah, I saw it."

"And you don't have any idea what that might have meant."

"None. Honestly. By that point, she was already a different woman to me."

Dan nodded. "Thank you again, Mr. Beal."

"No problem. Good luck."

Dan scrolled through recent suicide cases on his work computer, looking for Amanda's; he wanted to see if the toxicology was logged in her file. He tapped the toggle bar and scrolled until a chipper female voice interrupted him.

"Hey, Detective Winters," Eunice said giddily.

He looked up from his computer and almost winced. If Chief saw her over here, he would suspect Dan was conducting his own detective work. It had been a problem in the past. He may have called Dan Magic Man, but he didn't believe in hocus pocus.

"Hey, Eunice." Dan kept his voice quiet and light, hoping she would go away before Chief arrived. If not, he'd find some other way to occupy Dan's time. Like mountains of paperwork. "What's up?"

"We finished the toxicology," she said, inviting herself to sit across from his desk. "She didn't have any cannabinoids in her system. If she was on any drugs, they were out of her system, although she did have a trace amount of alcohol. There was also potassium cyanide." Dan's eyes flashed up to Eunice and she nodded. "Yeah. She killed herself twice."

Dan shook his head. "Why—no, how would anyone do that?"

Eunice breathed deeply and shrugged. "I don't know, detective. That's more your department."

"Okay. But Eunice, when you tell Chief Brigham about the injection site and the cyanide, uh, will you please not mention that it was my hunch?"

Eunice shook her head at him. "Why wouldn't you want credit?"

"I don't know. Call it another hunch."

"No skin off my nose."

She walked away, her spike heels clicking on the tile floor. Dan glanced back at his computer monitor, specifically to the clock at bottom of the screen: it was after five, time to go home. He hovered the mouse arrow over the X in the upper-right corner, preparing to close the app, when something in the ribbon at the top of the page caught his eye.

The file name: Branden Bullard.

"Branden Bull-something," Jermaine had said.

It was him, the link to Amanda Turner's other life.

But what was he doing here, with all the other recent suicides?

3
SPLITTING AT THE SEAMS

So, Amanda's friend, Branden Bullard, had also killed himself. And he'd done it the night of the gala.

Without a second thought to his plan to go home, Dan clicked on the name. The file sprang up onto his screen. Branden Bullard, twenty-six years old. Cause of death: trauma to the brain. Jumped from the top of the castle at the Eden Hope playground.

Dan leaned closer. Who in his right mind would jump from the top of a playground structure? Why would anyone want to leave that gruesome smear on a play place? Why hadn't he seen this one or heard about it … at all?

"Winters," Chief Lester snapped from behind, pulling Dan out of his thoughts. "I got back a toxicology on the Turner body."

"Oh?" Dan panned in his swivel chair, attempting to affect an air of ambivalence. "Anything interesting?"

"You know damned well what I'm talking about," Chief said. "Eunice told me you twisted her arm for it."

Damn it, Eunice! "Uh, I may have mentioned it. I just didn't want us to … to fail to exhaust all possible avenues, you know. Because Amanda was … someone's daughter. Someone loved her."

Chief stared at him for a beat or two, then nodded. "You're right about that," he conceded, turning to go.

"Hey, Chief," Dan called after him. For a split second, Dan weighed whether to confess that he'd been poking deeper into this closed case, and that he'd uncovered a link between Amanda Turner and Branden Bullard—but he hesitated. There wasn't enough yet. He didn't want to incur Chief's wrath until he knew for certain it was worthwhile. "Why didn't I attend the scene for this Bullard case? About ten days ago?"

"The Bullard case." Chief's eyes drifted, then they snapped into focus again. "Yes, the Eden Hope suicide. Ugh, that one." A visible chill seemed to shake Chief. "Initially, we classified that one as a homicide. The roommate said Bullard was on his way to meet someone at that playground. Thought maybe somebody pushed him. But, in the end, there were just too many missing pieces to call it a murder. No witnesses. Nothing in writing about a meeting. No trail to follow. And anyway, how could you convince a man to climb up on a rail like that and then jump?"

"What was his roommate's name?" The question popped out of Dan's mouth before he could stop himself, and he felt his eyes bulge slightly. Chief noticed, moved his bulk closer, and glowered down at Dan, who suddenly wished he wasn't stuck in this swivel chair like a fool.

"Don't you go digging around in cold cases just because you're bent out of shape about Amanda Turner," Chief Brigham said before strolling away. "The best thing we can do to help that girl now is track down her enemies, not waste time on dead ends. Focus, Magic Man!"

There was no mistaking Chief's meaning, but long after he had gone back to his office, the question lingered in Dan's mind: How could someone have forced Branden to jump from that height? Was it just the bad aftertaste of the Turner case driving him to tackle another hard-to-accept suicide? Dan only knew one thing: the best way to assess the likelihood that Branden Bullard had been forced to jump over the railing of the playground castle was to see the structure up close for himself.

It was late in the evening by the time Dan made it to Eden Hope playground. Despite the balmy evening weather and lingering rays of sunshine, the place was all but deserted. He pulled into the parking lot, noting only two other parked cars, although the playground itself was massive. Multicolored metal bars arched over the entryway as if beckoning children to come play, although Dan, not having been a kid for a long time now, only saw that the bars were beginning to rust.

The Plexiglas castle was immediately obvious, and not just because it towered at the playground's edge. It was also cordoned off with caution tape, and when Dan stepped closer and crossed it, he saw why.

There was a deep red stain on the earth. Resisting the urge to touch it, Dan crouched to glance up at the metallic spires. Yep, Chief was right. There was no way to explain how one adult man could force another adult man to climb and jump. Physics would be heavily on the side of the man being forced onto the rail. Even if he managed to climb it, he wouldn't have to jump.

Dan rose and tried to imagine Amanda's friend Branden here on the night of the gala. He remembered that night. He tried to see the man in his mind's eye, climbing through the castle, meeting somebody … And then what? He inhaled deeply, hoping to catch some errant clue through his nose ... like the deep, mellow fragrance of eucalyptus.

"Excuse me." A hesitant female voice interrupted Dan's thoughts, drawing him out of his process. It was her. She smelled of eucalyptus.

His eyes focused on a woman roughly his own age or slightly older. Her hair was thick and styled into a perfect blond bob. She had a petite face, and the sheer heaviness of the sorrow in her eyes seemed to pull every other feature downward. Everything about her orbited around those heartbroken cherrywood eyes.

"Wh—what are you doing here?" the woman asked.

Dan swallowed. He had seen this woman a thousand different times at a thousand different death scenes, across a thousand different strips of caution tape. They were always recognizable, not because of their age or appearance, but because of the eyes, gazing upon the space where their beloved, perfect child had perished.

"Please excuse me, ma'am," Dan said, his voice on autopilot. "I'm a police detective, Detective Winters, and I—" He wondered if she knew Amanda was dead. Jermaine had called them family friends, or something like that. Old friends?

"Well," he forged on, "I recently was assigned the suicide case of Amanda Turner, a friend of your son's, I assume? You're Branden's mother?" She nodded. "I wanted to explore—" He hesitated again. Damn it, he needed to get better at talking to people. He didn't want to give her false hope, but he'd already begun leading her into the sentence. Now he had nowhere else to go. Besides, if she knew, she had to have been thinking it too. "I wanted to explore the possibility of a connection between the two."

"You think so too?" She breathed out and extended her hand to him—no jewelry, not a speck of polish. Dan took it gently. "My name's Patricia, Patricia Camuzet."

"What a lovely name," Dan said, and meant it. He loved the French language. "Daniel Winters." They clutched hands for a moment, no shaking involved, before he released his and she took hers back, trembling. "Do you want to talk about it with me, Patricia? See if you can maybe give me any insight?"

She stared at him with eyes suddenly hardening. "I guess it's pretty simple," she said. "He was my firstborn. He did not have any addictions, to my knowledge. I was no longer sure of his sexuality, so I don't know who he was meeting. But I know of no reason he would have taken his own life." The words exploded out of her, as if from the bottom of her lungs, and she blinked those large, brown eyes at him. "I shouldn't be here." Fat tears rolled down her cheeks.

Dan reached forward and gently placed his hand on her arm. For a moment, he forgot about the case. "I know what you're going through. I mean, I lost my—my wife two years ago. I'm not saying you can compare the two, but—"

She watched him, like an animal measuring the approach of a human. Finally, her face relaxed a bit and she said, "I see what you're saying."

"You're right, you know," Dan said, taking his hand back. "I don't think you should be here. If you do want to talk about it with me, though, I'm here to listen."

Patricia stared at him for a moment before she took a deep breath and began. "He changed," she said simply. And with those two words, her torso caved inward, and her face puddled in the palms of her hands. She sobbed openly, and Dan put his arms around her, knowing it was the only thing a decent person could do. She let her initial burst finish out on his shoulder, but then pushed away from him softly and gazed at him with her features set somewhere between rage and sorrow: a warrior of quiet but total strength.

"It started in May. Mid-May. He came to visit, and he looked like a different person."

Dan's ears perked. This sounded like the same thing Jermaine had said about Amanda. He didn't speak. He sensed Patricia would say it all until she was finished.

"Changed his hair and his wardrobe. He was twenty-six. We knew him very well, obviously. He had never looked like this in his life. Very ritzy. Very loud, but in a fashionable way. Ugh, and the cologne!" Her eyes grew distant and glassy with another film of tears.

She was silent for a moment. Then she launched back into speech, her eyes still bright. "He would only speak in French. My family is from France, but I don't even speak French these days." She laughed—a husky, caustic sound—and continued. "But he was speaking in French. We asked if he'd met someone new, because, you know." She shook her head. "You don't just become a new person overnight for no reason at all. He said he was dating, but he was very vague about it." She hesitated. "And it wasn't just that."

"Oh?"

"He was … cold," she said slowly, as if forcing herself to say it, or perhaps trying to stop herself from saying it. "Something … had … changed. He mocked me for mispronouncing a word, and even—he even said it was a shame I'd abandoned our culture. It was hurtful. Snide. Arrogant. But that cologne was the worst. It was like he was trying to marinate himself."

"Would it be all right with you if I looked at Branden's apartment? Amanda Turner's boyfriend, or ex-boyfriend, Jermaine Beal, said something very similar to me, of his experience with Amanda shortly before she ended her life." He paused before adding, "If it was a suicide, that is."

Patricia's eyes narrowed, and her mouth reset into a thin, hard line. "Absolutely," she whispered, pressing keys into his palm until it hurt.

Branden's apartment was in the thick of the city, stacked on top of five other apartments that were no doubt identical to it. The sun radiated off the sidewalk, making the air seem to vibrate. Every window gleaming on the brick wall hung wide open, fans whipping. The central air system must have been down—had probably burned itself out. Dan paused on the sidewalk as sweat budded and dripped down his temple. He closed his eyes and savored the light aroma of a particular Australian vintage. Had someone spilled a bottle of Coonawarra on their countertop, leaving behind a red splash, not unlike the scene of Branden Bullard's plummet? He was sure of it. He could smell the characteristic eucalyptus note.

Entering the building was like stepping into an oven. Unseen cables pulled the elevator up six flights, where the doors slid open. As he strode down the hall to the Bullard apartment, the smell of Coonawarra grew stronger. When he opened the door, the scent wafted onto him in a hot, dry breeze, almost as if he had stepped onto an Australian Coonawarra vineyard at high noon.

Like Amanda's apartment, this space was small, and there was a feeling in the air as if the occupant had only just stepped out, as if things around the room had been left half-finished and any minute Branden would burst in, gushing apologies. Unlike Amanda's apartment, this place had an impeccable, almost austere feel to it, as if those inhabiting it performed regular chores but lacked the time or whimsy for decorating. A large bookcase displayed lots of limited editions. Someone had been very well read.

On top of the bookcase, just like at Amanda's house, bowls had been set out, like some kind of altar to a god. Withering black plums. Cherries. Dried violet petals.

Dan raked his fingers through it, trying to connect the two even here, even by this tenuous thread. What was it? Where was the connection between the fruit in the bowls? Was there a connection?

But he was—

He dipped his nose toward the bowl and brought it in deeply.

Hadn't Amanda's apartment reminded him of—

"Not you too." A male voice greeted Dan from behind. He turned swiftly and found himself face to face with a large young man with classic Nordic features, from the unforgiving jawbone to the lumpy nose. His shoulders were as broad and muscled as if he were an actual Viking, though Dan figured he probably just hit the gym very regularly. "He was obsessed with those bowls."

"Excuse me," Dan said to the young man. "I'm Detective Winters, just here to give the case a little more thought. The Bullards extended their permission for it, but I guess I should have made sure that it was okay with Branden's … roommate?"

The man shrugged. "I'm Matt," he replied, brusque and almost uninterested. "To tell the truth, man, Branden and I got matched by a roommate finder service. Neither of us smoke, both very clean, same age, looking in the same area, so they just kind of put us together, but I didn't know him well at all. So, you can look around, but I can't tell you much."

"I'm sure that's not true," Dan said as kindly as he could. "Did Branden ever bring anyone else by the apartment, or talk about them?"

"I work all the time, detective. And he didn't really entertain here. Sorry I can't be a bigger help. I'm going to hit the shower but let me know if you need anything. Uh, no one has been by to take his stuff, and I didn't want to just throw it away, so there's that." Matt shrugged again and made his way toward a bathroom accessible through the den. "His room is on the left at the end of that little hall." Matt pointed and Dan followed his direction, leaving him to shower in peace.

Branden's bedroom didn't give away much either. The drawers were neat and filled with regular clothes. The bed was made. The desk had drawers filled with common things: paper clips, old pay stubs from a retail store. Branden didn't seem to be sentimental at all. Dan powered on the computer, his last hope, but as the screen came to life, a security prompt popped up, its cursor blinking, field blank.

Dan settled and furrowed his brow, wondering how hard password guessing might be. First, he tried a combination of simple, obvious data that he could remember from Branden's file, like his last name and birth year. The computer grunted at him electronically. Wrong. He tried several combinations with no success—grunt, wrong, grunt, wrong—and grimaced, pushing his shoulders against the cushion of the computer chair and slumping. He let his mind drift, and the reminiscent notes of Branden's potpourri filtered back into his consciousness.

Screw it. Why not?

Dan straightened up, typed "Coonawarra," and hit ENTER. Instead of a grunt, there was a happy little "bing" as the computer let down its digital barrier, allowing Dan to see the desktop. He rifled immediately through recent documents, finding lots of cover letters and old essays, before trying the chat history logs.

He clicked on the only file from the night of Branden's death: a conversation between Branden (handle: Bully) and Google username Raymond Vasquez (handle: icy22).

icy22 (8:37 pm): I think we need to talk

Bully (8:48 pm): can't talk right now, about to go out

icy22 (8:49 pm): I'm serious, we need to talk TONIGHT

Bully (9:03 pm): I'll try to come by later

DAN CHEWED his lip and stared at the monitor. Branden's meeting that night might have been with Raymond. Could this be the same individual who'd become Amanda's obsession? If they were connected, was the killer still out there? How had they forced a healthy man to leap to his death? Dan swallowed, thinking of different ways to stage a suicide.

"You better get out," a male voice said from behind him.

He jumped, searching for the source. Matt, Branden's roommate, was leaning in the open doorway of Branden's bedroom, staring at him.

Dan stared back. "What?"

"You figured it out,'" Matt said. "His password. You figured it out."

Yes … Coonawarra. An Australian wine. The thread just keeps getting longer and more intriguing.

"Yes," Dan said. "I should be getting back to the station, but I'm going to leave my contact information here. I want you to get in touch if anything out of the ordinary happens."

Back at the station (even though he really should have gone home), Dan first went to the evidence locker for everything related to the Bullard scene that had been pulled. The only thing inside, however, was a leather backpack. It appeared that the contents had been separated and organized into labeled plastic bags, forming a microcosm of the same sensory notes from his apartment: the dried plums, cherries, and violets. Why had he brought them in his backpack?

Dan entered Raymond Vasquez's name into the system and pulled his record. He didn't know what he was looking for; this man probably was not the one. A vague thread of France was here, but Vasquez was Spanish. In Amanda's farewell message on Facebook, she had said, *bonjour*, and Branden's mother had noted his sudden interest in their mother tongue. Might the killer have been French?

Still, he sifted through the file for any information it had to offer about Branden's friend, the one who had needed so badly to talk to him on the night of his suicide. Raymond was thirty-three, a sensitive-looking man with shaggy, brown hair and hazel eyes. His address was also in the Bay area; a long-distance stakeout via Google Earth showed a man who stayed in a rather luxurious, classic-1970s, ranch-style home. Its lawn was decorated with plumes of grass at varying heights, the rest of the yard manicured to a perfect inch of fresh green. Its tones were amber and chocolate, creating an intimate, warm feel that drew the weary spirit onward.

But it was already dark outside, and Dan hadn't eaten since lunch, so he closed down his desk for the day and went home rubbing his eyes. He needed to take care of himself at some point. Someone had to.

Dan poked at the cold remnants of his wilted asparagus. His hand had been a little too heavy when he'd been spicing the thing, but it wasn't half bad. He cracked a smile at the limp finger of vegetable, remembering the stunt Kristin Meyers had pulled at her sommelier exam. During a pairing exercise, she'd chosen to contrast her aged sake with Canadian smoked meat and asparagus. Simple but genius. He shook his head. He couldn't believe it had been ten years.

Hell, no: it had been almost fifteen years! And how long had it been since he'd actually seen Kristin? Annie's funeral, now that he thought about it. She was a very pretty girl—back then, anyway, when all the girls were beautiful—with thick, wavy hair, a rich shade of auburn, skin like honey, and laughing eyes. He couldn't recall the color, but he remembered thinking she was always showing off her dimples.

He'd never pursued her, of course. Maybe part of him knew he was going to meet Annie, but another part had found Kristin's vivacious attitude a little terrifying. Dan had met Annabelle not long after failing his sommelier exam. At the time, he'd been furious, felt boxed in, fuming with resentment. Annie had helped him let go—helped him accept that, in some ways, he was an outsider, always would be, and there was nothing wrong with that.

Perhaps Dan remembered Kristin so vividly because she too was an outsider, but she was much less sensitive about it. While Dan enjoyed his solitude and guarded himself against the rest of the world (as much as it resisted him), Kristin was invasive and brave, the kind of girl who could shamelessly wear paint-splattered sneakers to a charity ball. The kind of girl who could giggle loudly in the middle of dinner prayer and get away with it.

He wondered what she was doing now. She had gone on to become a professional sommelier, and he thought he remembered hearing that she was now working at some fusion restaurant downtown, somewhere they would be impressed when they heard words like "unconventional" and "a little crazy." He thought the name of the bar was The House. He'd been there before, but not in a while. There was usually quite a wait, and the wine list was phenomenal.

Was he crazy to follow his nose on this one? Was he crazy to think these suicide scenes had attempted to mimic the bouquets of wines?

He wasn't sure, but there might have been a reason he'd thought of her tonight, gazing at this hopelessly overcooked spear of asparagus. Perhaps she could help.

Everything following dinner tended to be a blur for Dan. It had been that way for a while. With no one else in the house, he almost faded out. That was why his dinners with Boris and Rachel were such a touchstone—and what was today? How long had it been since he'd shared a meal with someone who cared about his day? At least a week. He rubbed his blurry eyes. He just didn't have the energy to keep track of everything anymore. Was that a hallmark of depression? Dinners were simple, monotonous, and painfully small. He had it boiled down to the perfect plate: portion of protein, portion of carbs, and some fruit or vegetable combination. Most nights, he didn't require more than a slab of chicken, half a cup of rice, and a handful of strawberries or zucchini.

After that there wasn't much left to do. He would take a shower. The sun would set. Something would come on television. Yes, some nights, he felt a vague shame, as if he was supposed to be getting out there. But that feeling was fleeting. A glass of wine, his most comfortable quilt, and a good murder mystery on TV would satisfy him the way nightclubs and starlit beaches inspired other people. Those things weren't so fun alone. And he was forty-two now. The world wasn't exactly alien, but it was ugly. He didn't want to drift in that sludge, just looking for something to grab onto.

He didn't go to sleep consciously thinking of Annie, but she was always lingering in the backyard of his thoughts.

They had wanted to backpack through the historic wine regions of Europe again for their second honeymoon. That was before Annie became ill, before even her breathing changed. She couldn't hold onto a single ray of sunshine, couldn't soak up a single pound. Europe, wine, everything faded. Annie devoted all her energy to the mysterious injection cocktail she was perfecting. She was sure she had it.

Dan thought of how that trip might have been if she had lived just two more years, so they could have made it to ten as a married couple. Then he realized that she had been gone for exactly two years, which would have made this year's anniversary their tenth.

He drifted off to sleep thinking of exploring the fragrant hills of Italy and France, and Annie, walking just ahead of him, wearing all white. Her backpack was somehow transparent, almost nonexistent, and seemed to carry nothing but bare light inside—or was that somehow her center, shining through the sheer fabric? Dan blinked and the entire satchel seemed to disappear. His eyes darted to the vineyard floor—had she dropped it? He didn't see it in the tall grass, didn't see anything but the darting flashes of Annie's bare feet, moving swift and graceful, one after the other. Why would she be barefoot while they were backpacking? She had lost her backpack and now her shoes. Dan had to find her shoes.

Annie glanced over her shoulder at him, her platinum blond hair falling in thick, disheveled waves of rough morning hair, the kind of hair that doesn't really have bounce or shine, but it's real. She looked like she'd just rolled out of bed. Her crystal blue eyes were brighter than usual. They practically glowed as she grinned and pulled him down the row of thick, writhing vines. Her whole body glowed, for that matter.

Dan blinked hard and looked closer.

These weren't vines. They were trunks, their torsos, stretched, contorted and gray, their faces and hair the head and buds. The first was Amanda Turner, her withered curls a stiff explosion around her cheeks, like the leaves of a vine. Dan leaned closer to examine her. Her face seemed peaceful but shrunken. Was she dead?

Her eyes opened and trained on his. He pulled back with a jerk, and she blinked up at him, somber and silent.

He didn't think she could move. He reached out to touch her hair, and several almonds dropped from the strands, which turned out to be branches. He swallowed and leaned close again, noticing a mélange of rotten fruit oozing from her bark: peaches and honeysuckle, bitter almonds. It grew more potent as it saturated his skin, a part of him flourishing as he savored the intoxicating bouquet.

Dan took a step back as Annie's voice called him. Are you coming? She didn't say the words, but he knew she was thinking them. She gazed at him, then looked over her shoulder—at a massive, soft white light in the distance. It wasn't glaring or hurting his eyes, but he couldn't discern where the glow was coming from.

He took a step with Annie, toward the light, and her excitement was palpable. Her hands were all over him, her eyes alive, but Dan hesitated as they passed another vine. This one was Branden Bullard. His vine was steeped in a dark red Australian soil, and when Dan leaned closer to him, he caught all the flavors of the palate: plums, cherries, violets.

Annie pulled him away. The light was starting to fracture and dim.

Dan went with her another few steps, his feet heavier and slower; he wanted to be with her, but he wanted to stay and examine this vineyard more closely too. Could the key to the Turner and Bullard cases be tucked here, in this ethereal place? Another tree was coming up, also gray and twisted. A human tree, waiting for him—who was it? Who was next?

He advanced on it, but again felt a tug. Annie was waiting for him at the threshold of the light. It swirled as if to welcome him, even as it shrank away from him. Dan looked at the new tree, then at Annie, then back to the tree again, torn between destinies.

Looking back at Annie once more, he saw that she and the light were both beginning to fragment. Dan was taking small steps backward. The light split apart and faded away before he made it to the new tree. The world went dark.

Dan's eyes opened to the lightless ceiling overhead.

4
BIRTH AND DEATH

The tension created by that weird nightmare hung around Dan like a shroud for the rest of the weekend. As he watched TV and ate his small, lonely dinners, he thought about the new tree in that vineyard of flesh. Who was it? Dan never used to be superstitious, but since that dream, he couldn't look at his own face in the bathroom mirror without recalling the way Amanda's shrunken head had gazed up at him, blank, as he touched her almond-filled hair. Who else was at risk? Matt, Branden's roommate? Patricia, his mother?

Dan swallowed and his eyes bore into his reflection. The water in the sink continued to run, and toothpaste dripped from his toothbrush.

He supposed he could be at risk too. He had visited the scenes of both alleged suicides, and if this was indeed a serial killer, that criminal profile alone suggested a likelihood of the perpetrator returning to the scenes of the crimes, watching the detectives at work.

What if that had been the meaning of the swirling light, of Annie calling him onward? Was his time on this case—or even on this Earth—coming to a close?

He tried not to let it get to him. Life was crazy, and sometimes you got murdered. Annie would have said he was being melodramatic. Did cops sometimes die on the job? Yes, but traffic cops were at more risk than detectives. He remembered a day a few years back when an officer from another division had a close brush during an arrest. It had set every cop in the city on edge. One morning a few days later, Annie was reading an op/ed about the incident. The reporter, married to a cop and worried that anxious coworkers didn't make his wife's job safer, cited statistics showing that more retail workers were murdered on the job than cops.

Retail workers. Dan could still hear Annie's voice telling him to take a breath, let it go, and drive to work.

It was still good advice. Besides, what other choice did he have?

As he crossed the parking lot toward the police station, his gait slowed, and he frowned at the waiting glass doors. He didn't see anyone inside. It was Monday morning. They should have been bustling about; there was bound to be a backlog of paperwork left over from the weekend, wasn't there?

He opened the foyer door, but then hesitated. Typical odors mingled in the air: the rubber of rushing shoe soles, the fresh peel of warm printer paper, even all the different colognes and perfumes fighting for dominance. It signaled to Dan that live men and women had just been in here. But there was something else. Something tiding almost on top of the air, too foul to be a part of it.

Smoke. Smoke on the air. Fire.

Possibilities raced through Dan's subconscious like a spark along a fuse. What if the killer was in the station? What if there was a bomb?

His blood pressure skyrocketed as he launched himself through the hall, gripping the second set of glass doors that led into the actual ground floor of the station, yanking each open—and smelling the accompaniment to the smoke too late.

Wax. Cheap wax.

Suddenly, two dozen figures sprang up from behind their desks, hollering, "Happy birthday, Detective Winters!" Dan fell back a step and placed a hand over his heart, only half kidding. Chief's office door opened and the large man swaggered out, bearing a pink-and-white frosted cake in his hands. Forty-three candles blazed on its surface, threatening to melt the cake along with the wax.

Dan shook his head warily. He hadn't even realized today was the day. He'd thought it was later this week, or perhaps it had already passed. He wasn't sure—in his mind, it was a moving target—but he hadn't thought it was today, and he had never imagined the precinct would put together an actual cake and surprise party for him.

"Didn't see this one coming, did you, Magic Man?" Chief boasted. "Gonna need your nose deeper in those coffee beans next time, huh!"

"They were Harrar—" Dan began, immediately realizing his mistake: the assumption that Chief cared.

"All right, kids, everybody calm down," Chief said, purposely ignoring Dan. "Let's all shut up and eat cake for just a minute." He brandished a chef's knife and began slicing.

And for a few wild minutes of childlike bliss, two dozen of some of the thickest-skinned souls in San Francisco—men and women who had rescued children from real-life monsters, who had seen people kill over a boundary crossed or a color worn—moseyed around, digging with plastic forks into pieces of buttercream vanilla birthday cake balanced on blue cardboard saucers and laughing together.

Then the phone rang, and within seconds, the room filled with the soft crinkle of plastic as half-eaten pieces of cake were dumped into trash cans and napkins wiped away any colorful, sugary evidence that this event had taken place at all.

"You've got another scene to attend in Niles," Chief informed Dan.

"In Niles?" Why did that sound familiar? Oh, shit.

"Gunshots," Chief answered, letting Dan know he was hardly listening at all. "A Raymond Vasquez found in his living-room recliner. No signs of forced entry."

Chief handed Dan some paperwork to take with him to the scene, but it wasn't the paperwork he was really trying to give Dan. The imperative look in his eye told Dan the real message was here, between them.

"Don't try to get all fancy with this one," Chief commanded.

Dan swallowed the urge to question his use of the word "fancy." What did that even mean? Instead, he answered, "I won't," because he knew exactly what Chief meant: No frills. No unnecessary investigating.

But Dan knew something Chief did not—that Ray Vasquez had wanted to talk to Branden Bullard on the night Bullard had died.

The lens through which Dan had seen the Vasquez home only two nights earlier now seemed fuzzy with optimism. He had thought it looked warm and inviting. But when he had been looking at Google Earth street view, a living man had occupied the space. Now, as Dan climbed out of his car and trod toward the Niles rancher, he saw a totally different house, a house he knew was empty inside. The doors and windows would be open for now, the place abuzz with activity. Once the police were done, a realtor or landlord would come and close it up. It would sit, dark and quiet, for months. The furniture would disappear in an auction. Then someone would buy the house, move in, and put their recliner in this living room, perhaps right where Raymond Vasquez had shot himself.

North and Manozza had already parked their cars and gone inside, so Dan strode through the open door, across a wide swath of butter-colored tiles, and past a straight shot of long, vertical windows gazing out onto an in-ground pool. He hadn't mentioned to anyone that he'd already seen this house, albeit on a computer screen, that he'd already seen this man, sort of, or that he'd almost known there would be another suicide … death under abnormal circumstances … murder?

Could he have done more? What if he hadn't been so tired on Friday evening? What if he had come here instead, and interviewed Vasquez? Would anything have changed?

Crossing the threshold into the room where Vasquez's body still lay, he reeled at the odor of fresh blood, which dominated everything else. The corpse had not yet been removed, and unlike Amanda's, it was not old. This had happened within the hour, so the stench was pure copper.

The man was stretched out in the recliner, his face unrecognizable, a gaping maw of gore. He appeared to be naked except for a purple crushed-velvet robe, which had shrugged open and left the corpse looking like a drunk man, fresh from the Jacuzzi. Sloppy, unaware.

Yet even stronger than the smell and the gore was a particularly acrid undertone of burnt rubber that seemed to permeate the premises. Dan followed the foul odor to the patio, where he found the glass door open and the barbecue turned on. A strip of tire rubber had been laid across the grill alongside burnt venison, scorched and bloody at the same time, with shriveled olives and melted packets of dark chocolate. The plastic hadn't even been removed from the chocolate. It was maniacal, and it reminded him of something—the same meticulous obsession with detail at Amanda's apartment—the prosciutto, the walls, the rope. And at Eden Hope playground, the way Branden had cherries and plums in his backpack.

Why was every little detail so important? Were the victims crafting these bizarre bouquets of scent, or was it the killer?

"You guys seen this?" Dan called through the open glass door.

"No," they called back in unison.

A few seconds passed, and Dan heard boots stomping across the floor. Juan Manozza's shadow fell across the patio. "Shit," he muttered. Globs of burnt chocolate sizzled on the grill. The tire strips fumed madly. "That's crazy."

"Does this remind you of the Turner scene in any way?" Dan said.

Juan gazed back at him and nodded somberly. "People who die by suicide aren't supposed to care anymore. But these two cared very much. The body —Vasquez—he's covered in pepper. It looks like he rubbed it all over himself. All in his hair, over his hands." Juan shuddered. "It doesn't make sense."

Dan nodded and swallowed.

These scents had been in his glass a couple of weeks ago. A coincidence? Most certainly. How could it be anything else? The night Branden Bullard had killed himself, Dan had been savoring the peppery undertones of his own deep burgundy Syrah, the color almost a precise match to the robe on the body in the recliner.

But then, what about the Friulano?

The smell of Amanda's apartment, the perfect pairing with the prosciutto, and even the walls painted to match its tone. The handwoven rope—suddenly, like magic, the memory that had been tickling at the edge of his consciousness was there for him to snatch. He recalled where he'd seen it before. On his honeymoon with Annie, they'd backpacked across the Slovenian-Italian border, through the sleepy city of Udine, where the rare white grapes of the Friulano grew. On those streets were the basket weavers they had seen, and the rope had been woven in that style.

And then, there was the strange leap of Branden Bullard, whose computer password was "Coonawarra." He'd dashed himself on red granite like the soils of an Australian vineyard, carried the elements of Coonawarra in his backpack, been obsessed with the odors—and with his mother's family's first language.

Why?

Why France? Why the wines? The entire rancher stank of Côte Rôtie, another nod to France, made in the Rhône Valley, just south of Vienne, a small town by Lyon, where tiny, writhing trees populated the steep hills. He remembered the taste of the Syrah in his glass on that trip. He'd paired his with a rare steak, but the venison made sense too.

Juan shrugged, swore off the confusion of this scene, and made his way back to Barry, leaving Dan staring into the pillar of vile exhaust.

It didn't make any sense to Juan—but it made perfect sense to Dan. Was it just a coincidence that he was a connoisseur, and that these suicides—or murders, as he was increasingly believing they were—mimicked the flavors and pairings of wine? Was he the only person on this force who could stop San Francisco from seeing a fourth murder inside a month? The worst part was that he had known this was happening, but he hadn't believed in it. He'd seen an omen of another murder, and his theory was forming a shape, but he hadn't taken it to Chief yet because he'd known the man wouldn't accept it. Dan would have been laughed out of the station.

But Vasquez was dead now. Dan knew he couldn't hold his tongue another day.

5
KRISTIN'S WORLD

His meeting with Chief went precisely as expected.

"Look, Winters." Chief shook his head and grinned at the apparently misguided detective. "The cyanide in Turner's system has reopened the case as a potential homicide. I'll give you that; you had a solid hunch, Magic Man. But the meat on the rug, the paint on the walls—"

"It's all part of a greater picture," Dan insisted. He wasn't normally the type to force an issue, but this time it mattered. He had to make Chief see. "Amanda and Branden knew each other. Amanda might have even known Ray."

"Who?"

"Turner and Bullard were friends," Dan said, huffing. "Ray Vasquez also knew Bullard. He may have known Turner as well."

Chief's brow dented. "How did you come by that information? Why is this the first I'm hearing of it?"

Dan shook his head. "I found out last week when I made a private call to Amanda Turner's ex-boyfriend. He mentioned Bullard to me, and then I saw Bullard's file." Dan wanted to stop there, and wished he could, but if his theory was going to make any sense, he had to tell Chief everything. "I went to the scene of the crime."

Chief exhaled like a bull. "On my time?"

Dan nodded, grim, expectant of his fate. "I met his mother, she was there, and she gave me permission to look in his apartment."

"Oh, really?" Chief crossed his arms over his chest and nodded. His eyes were flat and void of amusement, but he pursed his lips and said, in a deadly tone, "I'm gonna let you finish."

"The password to his computer was 'Coonawarra,' a particular Australian wine that's—" he paused, knowing how this would sound to Chief, "that's famed for growing in dark red soil. Just like the granite top of the playground."

Chief raised his eyebrows as mirth bubbled out of his gut. He shook his head and hunched over, bowing down toward his desk. "You're telling me you want to call Bullard's case a murder because of the color red?" Despite the laughter, a palpable frustration was coming off him. "Do you know how much shit in this city is red, Dan? I mean, come on. What are you thinking? So, you guessed his password, and it was some fruity drink. So what? I'm going to need more than that."

"Yeah? Well, how about this. On that computer, on the night of his death, Branden had a conversation with Ray Vasquez. Ray said they needed to talk. I don't know if they ever saw each other, but I do know something was happening. And then Branden and Ray were both dead."

Chief exhaled and continued to shake his head at Dan. "I still don't see the firm connections you're seeing, but I'll concede there's likely more here than meets the eye. We'll have to reopen all three." His gaze was not approving. "You should have brought this to me last week, Winters," he barked. "You're not a vigilante. You're part of a team. We might not support your theory, but that doesn't justify hoarding discoveries so you can solve these equations with only your own formula in mind. That's not fair. It's not fair to the city, to your coworkers, to the families, or to the victims."

A pain sank through Dan's chest and into the pit of his stomach as Chief spoke. He hadn't thought of it that way. He just liked working alone.

"We'll reopen the cases," Chief repeated, "but this wine tip is your own business, Winters. Don't slow down the investigation trying to connect dots that aren't there."

Dan scanned the log on his cell phone as he trudged up the walk to his home. He'd missed a call from Boris at 6:30, probably checking to see if he'd like to join for dinner. How long had it been? It could have been two weeks, but Dan couldn't help it. This case was invading his mind, leaving him with only vestiges of genuine sleep. Evening had fully descended, and his knees ached, but he still wished he could socialize a little bit before sleep overtook him.

Shuffling for his keys in his pocket in the twilight, he almost didn't see the large cardboard box on his stoop until he was on top of it. He looked up from his keys and went still. There it was. Just sitting there.

Dan frowned. He couldn't remember ordering anything.

Oh, yes, he recalled now. He'd ordered some cookware. It was supposed to be a nine-pan set, so the dimensions of the box were a little smaller than he'd expected, but then again, he didn't know how efficiently they might have packed it all in. He just hoped this box contained the sautéing pan. He could make sweet pepper frittatas in the morning.

He straddled the box to unlock the door, then hoisted it into his arms and carried it to his kitchen, resting it gently on the counter and going to hunt for a knife. He scored the tape apart and stretched the stiff top flaps open. Reaching inside, he thought he would grip the handle on a pan and pull it loose, but there were no handles. There was only the cool, smooth glass of three bottles.

Dan extracted them one at a time, examining them in the light. The first was an earthy, rich, red, labeled Coonawarra. The second, a Rhône Valley Syrah. The last, a Friulano.

He pulled the last bottle out, ducking his head as if expecting a bomb to explode, but nothing happened. There was nothing further inside the box save one small note on a folded tab of stiff, creamy parchment. A minimalist prickling of filigree bordered the edges. The message inside was handwritten in spiky black cursive, at once delicate and wild. It read, "*Bon appétit.*"

A chill ran down Dan's spine. It couldn't be, but it was true; he had been right this whole time. Someone was murdering to recreate wine bouquets, and they were showing him privately, right now. But why? And how were they choosing the victims? And what wine would be part of the next fatal pairing?

Gooseflesh rose on his arms as he slowly put the bottles back in the box.

The killer knew where he lived. The killer was watching. The killer even knew that Dan knew and was sending him bottles of wine to taunt him.

Guess I need an enhanced home security system, Dan thought.

❆

Dan went for a drive. The horizon drank the sun, exhaling deep orange vapors across the clouds. By the time he had waded through the traffic leading into the city, the sky had evolved into a psychedelic starburst of indigo and lavender—beautiful, but only made possible by extreme air pollution.

He wasn't sure where he was going. He just had to get away from his house. Every window seemed to darken with the killer's shadow. He would have to go back at some point tonight.

When Kristin's restaurant rose up in his windshield, he knew he was going to talk to her. He pulled over and parked. She might not even be scheduled for tonight, he thought. Maybe she doesn't even work here anymore. He didn't know.

But it didn't matter. He could enjoy a small plate at the bar—perhaps they sold frittatas here—and, most importantly, he could avoid going home for as long as possible. He climbed out of the car, and even though he was on the street and the restaurant was on the fourth floor of this building, he could smell what a beginner might classify as "rotten meat." But Dan knew better.

He traveled up four flights, and sure enough, the odor grew stronger as he drew closer. When he pushed open the front door, it rolled over him in a swath.

A man in a smart tuxedo grinned expectantly at Dan. "Good evening, sir," he chirped. "Do you have a reservation with us tonight?"

"Uh, actually, I don't know if I need a table. I really just need to speak with a member of your staff. Would that be possible?"

The host considered Dan. Something about his demeanor must have spoken of official business, because the other man conceded quickly. "Who is it?"

"Your sommelier, Kristin Meyers. Is she on duty tonight?"

"Oh, yes. She's here every night except Sunday. Would you like her to recommend a pairing for you? I can squeeze you onto a seat at the bar until she's ready."

"Actually we're old friends. Could you let her know that Daniel Winters is asking for her? Maybe she would allow me back into the kitchen; it's a very private and critical matter. I'm Detective Daniel Winters," he said, which always tended to lend him a few thousand pounds of credibility. "And, if it's not too much trouble, I'd love to—" How best to put this? There was no easy way to encapsulate it in a sentence, so he bailed and said "—to catch up with her."

"Of course. Give me one moment."

The host vanished into the back of the restaurant. The dining room was not as packed as Dan had expected. Granted, it was late on a Monday, but this was a five-star place. The host reappeared and gestured him forward through a swinging wooden door propped open. As Dan passed through, he swiped at the doorstop wedge with his foot, kicking it away and closing the door to the kitchen.

Durian. That was what he'd smelled. The odor was overpowering now, in the very bowels of this beast. Cooks scurried back and forth, but there was one still point in the background.

Unlike Dan, Kristin had not aged much in the past fifteen years at all. Even less in the past two years, since he'd briefly seen her—he thought he remembered that anyway, although the entire service was a blur—at Annie's memorial. Her hair spilled down to her shoulders now, long, thick, and wavy, like Annie's had been. But, aside from being the same age, Kristin and Annie looked nothing alike.

Whereas Annie's face had been a classic oval sweep, soft chin, and delicate cheekbones, Kristin's was a vivacious heart shape, with full cheeks and a whittled chin. Her nose was pert and girlish where Annie's had been aristocratic, womanly. Her figure was generous, but Dan didn't allow his gaze to shift from her face. She wore a white button-down blouse and a black pencil skirt.

"Daniel Winters," she breathed, a slow smile perking at her lip. She leaned more heavily onto one side of her hip and her dimple deepened. "Whatever are you doing in my house?"

"The smell of that durian pulled me in," Dan joked. He slid his hands over the counter and tried to make himself look like he felt comfortable here. Like the world wasn't falling apart.

"I forgot about your nose!" She rolled her eyes upward, then back down to him, never breaking that unbeatable smile. "You must've been able to smell it all the way from your house."

Dan laughed with her. "Almost."

For a few seconds, they simply stared at each other, but just when it was about to get awkward, Kristin became animated again, nodding and springing on her heel.

"Let's move a little farther back, so that smell doesn't make you pass out—and so we can catch up." She gestured deeper into the kitchen, past a partition, and they moved away from the hubbub of closing time.

As they walked, Dan said, "So, Kristin, don't keep me in suspense. What will you pair with that durian?"

They entered another area lined with bottles of wine and refrigerators, with one metal island in the center of the room and some spare pots hanging over it. Metal counters running along the sides of the walls were stacked with clean plates, bowls, and silverware. They were alone here, and it was quiet. Kristin spread a hand over the metal island, perfectly relaxed. Considering all the bottles of wine, this was probably where she spent much of her time, and that apparently lent her comfort.

"You're asking me?" she wondered brightly. "I always thought you were the more gifted sommelier of the two of us, with that nose of yours. Do you use it in your line of work, Dan? Or do you still hide it from the world?"

Dan blushed a little. "I'm a police detective," he reminded her.

Kristin grinned. "I remember. You're like a bloodhound," she said. "The world's first ever forensic sommelier."

"I like that. But you know this old thing," he tapped at the side of his nose with his index finger, "can't compare to your creativity."

Kristin's sparkling eyes sobered up by a fraction. "Let's find out. What would you pair, Dan?"

"I would pick a Sauvignon Blanc, perhaps with some residual sugar, to go with your durian. Then it would be decidedly forgettable."

Kristin threw her head back in an unapologetic guffaw. "Boy, that would be ripe!"

She finished laughing and for a moment appeared to be critically examining the underside of a hanging pot. Dan only realized when she ran her fingers through her hair that she was checking her reflection. For him? That was silly. He was practically an old man in so many ways. Used up. Sad. A woman like Kristin still had the world at her fingertips. She had no need to impress ghosts like Dan Winters.

"To tell you the truth, when our head chef, Carlton, asked me if I could work with durian, I almost said no. I almost said it. But that only would have stemmed the genius."

"Oh?" Dan had to admit she'd piqued his curiosity. He was so intrigued by the vibrant way Kristin spoke of her work that he had almost forgotten about the killer.

"The fruit itself leaves little chance to isolate and highlight its amazing flavor," she said. "But you know what I thought?"

"What did you think?"

"If we could just chill the durian down, tame it, and streamline the flavor—highlight its strengths, diminish the weaknesses—then we could come up with a distilled essence. We were looking for something that mirrors the initial appeal of the durian but reduces its pungency." Kristin flounced over to the countertop and plucked a small spoon from a pile of them. She finished her proposition with a flourish, "Something that has all of nature's beauty and perfection in its composition."

"Ice cream?"

"Close! Sorbet."

Striding to one of the several large refrigerators lining the back of the kitchen, she struggled to open its massive door and then returned with a small cup of smooth yellow ice. She dipped the spoon into the scoop and held it out, floating it in front of Dan's nose. She was clearly having fun, seeing him again, and he was glad to see her too. He didn't know why, but in a sudden gesture he grabbed the spoon from her hand and ate the durian sorbet. If it bothered her, her expression gave nothing away.

"So, what do we do with it?" she said, her voice chirpy and melodic. "New world Sauvignon Blanc would be crazy; just because it's pungent doesn't mean it fits. The wine has to hold its own, but not interfere." She sifted through the bottles lining the wall, searching for the perfect pairing. As she looked, she spoke. "The world is a big place with big flavors. People may taste them while traveling, but many flavors stay put until discovered."

She pulled a bottle from the wall and whipped a corkscrew from what must have been her back pocket, inserting and twisting it. "I mean, when did you last see kaffir limes at a supermarket?" The corkscrew twirled in her hand. "I wanted to help these flavors travel too." The cork popped and she stood up straighter, wearing an unabashedly proud smile. "I expect you to pick up this odor from where you stand."

"Mmm, ahh." Dan closed his eyes, pulled deeply through his nose, and nodded to himself. "Durian and Hunter Valley Semillon."

He opened his eyes again and beheld Kristin with renewed appreciation. She was passionate and dedicated, but the real oomph came from how freely her mind could create. He had to admit that here in her kitchen, surrounded by wines and exotic foods, he envied her. "Could there be two more different worlds?" he asked her.

"Once you try them together, you'll be surprised nobody has tried this before. At least, not that I know."

Kristin snatched two wine glasses from over the counter, so subtly dangling that he hadn't even seen them, and returned, placing their feet on the island with a tiny clink. She poured a measure of Semillon into each and gestured for Dan to take his glass. He did so, and Kristin raised hers.

"To old friends," she toasted. The tips of their glasses sang together, and Dan repeated, "To old friends." They shared a smile and upended their glasses simultaneously.

The creamy durian sorbet, strange and sour, contrasted and flourished against the backdrop of the citrus sweetness in the Semillon—another Australian wine—with its notes of unripe lemon and grapefruit.

Dan nodded deeply and raised his glass again to toast Kristin. The woman was a genius. She'd said so herself and he was inclined to agree.

"I wish I could be a fly on the wall when your guests try it," he said.

"Or you could just come to dinner."

She said it so casually, as if each word just bubbled out of her. He could scarcely believe it. How was all this so simple for her, and so hard for him?

She settled her own glass with a clink on the island between them. "We're booked out months in advance, but dare I say you know the right people."

Dan felt a hint of warmth creeping into his cheeks. He hadn't expected this beautiful woman to flirt with him, but he quickly batted away a boyish discomfort that was brewing like active yeast in his stomach. He wasn't here for that, and that wasn't what this was, and anyway, Kristin was just a flirtatious woman. She probably made everyone feel this way, from the lowest busboy to the patrons themselves.

"Oh, I don't know," he gently declined. "I actually came on account of business, Kristin."

Her smile would not be vanquished. "Business?" Her eyes gleamed as though she'd never even heard that word before. "But you're a detective." Then the realization hit, and her gleam sputtered and died. So did her smile. "Did something happen?"

Dan reached forward and touched her arm, shaking his head. "We're still not quite sure."

"That's not a no."

"Within the past month, there have been three 'suicides' in the Bay area," he said, using air quotes.

"'Suicides'?" She air-quoted back, confused.

"They appear to be suicides, but I have … well, really strong doubts." He didn't want to tell her about the box of wines. He didn't want to scare her. "They all knew each other personally. All three had killed themselves in a specific setting, with a strong attention to the colors, flavors, and umm, pairings to their deaths."

Kristin's eyebrows knotted together. She leaned forward as if she couldn't have heard him right. "Pairings to their deaths?"

Dan nodded. "The first victim's room was decorated like an homage to Friulano with prosciutto di san Daniele spread out on the carpet."

"Oh my God." Kristin touched her manicured nails to her lips. "I don't know what to tell you, Dan. I don't—I don't understand. How can I help?"

"I need to know where he or she will strike next. I need someone who can get into the mind of a possible wine-loving serial killer."

"I would think either one of us could do that." Kristin cracked a wry smile. "But I do have some limitations. If you brought me your murder scene to sniff, I might be able to suggest a nice meal to accompany it."

Dan nodded and spread a hand on the countertop, grim and uncertain. "Maybe I just wanted to talk to someone about it. I need to—to understand." *Not to mention that I'm a little scared to sleep in my own bed tonight,* he thought to himself.

Kristin looked around as if someone might be watching them at this very moment. She lowered her voice. "You haven't told anyone? You know what's going on, and you haven't told anyone?"

"I did, but my chief wouldn't listen," he mumbled. "I'm alone."

Kristin's eyes went distant as she leaned her hip on the side of the island and ruminated. "I suppose I might be able to get you some interviews with a few wine experts I know. It's not much, but it's a start."

"You think you could?"

Kristin smiled tentatively. "Yeah." Her hand slithered across the counter and covered his with a warm pat. "You're not alone."

For a few beats, Dan got almost lost in her eyes. He stood up a little straighter and his breathing returned to normal. Had he stopped breathing for a second?

"I guess I should probably start helping them close the kitchen down," Kristin said reluctantly.

Despite how badly he did not want to be expelled back onto the street, with nowhere to go but home, he nodded and summoned a smile for her. "Of course. Thanks for making time for me tonight, Kris." He stuck his hand out for her to shake, but she stepped forward and wrapped her arms around his neck in a firm hug.

"Anytime, Dan." A little dazed, Dan brought his arm around her and patted her back, swallowing. He could still taste the queer combination of Semillon and durian sorbet on his tongue.

She stepped back and led him through the partition, giving him a small wave goodbye as he passed into the dining area. Then he was back down the elevator and onto the street, feeling as if he'd been spat from a brilliant world into a bleak one.

Kristin's domain was bright and warm and full of flavor and life, spirit and spirits. She wasn't afraid to approach a strange noise in the shadows; she didn't have to be. Her world was safe. He'd seen the way her smile and the light in her eyes dimmed at the mere mention of death, of crime. Her world was a happy bubble.

And his world—his world was this. Dark streets stretching out in every direction, waiting for the next call. The next body. Even his home offered no respite anymore.

Was it reprehensible of him to draw her into this? Could he live with himself if he popped her shiny bubble and stained her world with his?

6

DOWNTOWN HEART

Dan slept fitfully for the rest of the week, often waking to wander to his windows and peer out at the street, angry at himself for never getting around to installing a gate, as he'd often said he would. He religiously set the alarm system on all of his doors and windows—something he otherwise frequently forgot to do—and it gave him a fractional feeling of security. He was able to claim a few hours of sleep every night. He still didn't trust the shadows and the corners. But no boxes came, no murders cropped up.

It should have been the perfect opportunity to develop the three open cases, but as usual, this was a busy week in SFPD, and Chief wanted Dan's efforts concentrated elsewhere. It was enough to take up all his work hours. When Dan asked why he was being shunted to obvious, open-and-close suicides when he had put solid effort into the three open cases they had this month, Chief mumbled something about the validity of reopening those cases.

"What the hell are you talking about?" Dan snapped back. He knew Chief was his boss, but he couldn't school his tone fast enough. He could feel the pulse tapping in his neck too.

"Jesus Christ, Winters," Chief barked. He closed his office door and continued shouting. "It's possible that there is a real messed-up serial killer out there—"

"I know that!"

"—who is throwing people off castles and shooting cyanide into women's toes!"

Dan huffed wordlessly. The cyanide had been his find. These were his cases! How could Chief do this to him?

"And we need a dedicated homicide detective with enough common sense to put it together and give us a solid profile of this cat before another body turns up!"

"So, there it is," Dan growled. "You don't think I'm on the right track."

"I've been pretty honest about that. I never thought you were on the right track with this sicko."

"So, the cyanide wasn't my discovery?" Before Chief could respond, Dan hurried on. "What if I told you that the killer had personally sent a box of wines to my home—three wines, each one referenced at one of the murder scenes? What would you say to that?"

Chief stared at him, steely-eyed, and blinked with disregard. "I would say that you probably forgot about your subscription to some wine-of-the-month club."

Dan grimaced, stormed out of Chief's office, and got to work on the mountain of monotonous paperwork his boss had made sure would snowball onto his desk.

On Wednesday, Dan's phone chirped where it lay, face up on his desk, signaling the arrival of a text message. He was still filling out the paperwork from the first suicide of the day, a body that had just been returned from toxicology with a clean report.

Dan's brow furrowed. The number on his phone wasn't attached to a name. If the killer knew where he lived, he could easily find his cell number. He unlocked the phone and read the message.

Hey, I just wanted to let you know that I got in touch with some people and they're all available this Saturday, late morning/early afternoon, if you can do it then. This is Kristin, by the way.

Finally, a splash of sunshine in his week. Not because Kristin had sent him a message, or that she'd taken the trouble to hunt down his number through mutual acquaintances, although he warmed with pleasure at those thoughts. The beam of sunlight was because, whether Chief liked it or not, Dan was still deep in this case, and he wasn't letting go of his theory.

He didn't know why, and he didn't pause to think about it, but he continued to feel a warm spot in his chest as he saved Kristin's number to his phone.

Dan dropped a peach into his produce bag and placed it delicately in his grocery cart. He had the cherries, the plums, and some prosciutto, and was ambling toward a kiosk of fresh flowers when he recognized the narrow back of a brunette woman, carefully squeezing an avocado. Satisfied, she added it to her bag and turned. Her eyes lit on Dan, and she smiled.

"Hey, Dan," Rachel Porter said brightly, a spring in her step as she approached him. "What are the odds? How many people are supposed to live in this city?"

"About a million," Dan answered, blasé, then beamed. "But you're one in a million, kiddo."

"Flawless logic." Rachel came close for a quick hug, placing a hand at the base of his neck and giving an extra squeeze before pulling back again. "How are you doing? I haven't seen you in—jeez, I haven't seen you since the Friday night after Annie's gala." Rachel's cheeks burned bright pink. "I mean—not—you know—"

"I know what you mean," Dan said. If he got sore every time someone accidentally stepped on his heart, he wouldn't be able to make it to work in the morning. Annie was gone. He had accepted that. He had to.

"I guess it's been about three weeks, hasn't it?"

Rachel shook her head emphatically. "It feels like longer. How've you been? Boris will be jealous that he missed this."

"I miss you guys too," Dan said. "Work has just been really demanding lately." A half-truth was not always a lie; it was just easier than telling the whole truth. "It's Friday, isn't it? What are you guys making tonight?"

"Sweet potato ravioli with ricotta."

"Sounds delicious."

"I'm excited about it," Rachel said. "Hope it's not too challenging." Her eyes shifted to Dan's cart, then back to Dan. "What are you having for dinner? Fruit salad?"

"Uh, yeah." Another half-truth. They were piling up. "I should actually—"

"Oh!" Rachel yelped. "I remember now—" She lowered her voice to a hush. "Whatever happened with that suicide case?"

As much as Dan loved Rachel, she was one of those people who had no idea what the word "confidential" meant.

"You know—the body you sniffed?"

Dan nodded. He remembered the last time he'd seen Rachel and Boris, they'd enjoyed the Friulano and antipasto, and he had confessed his obsession with Amanda Turner's death.

"The case has been reopened as a homicide," Dan said. Rachel's eyes widened. "I've actually got a big interview with an expert coming up this weekend. I'm trying to recreate the sensory information from each scene, but it's proving difficult. Almost done, though. Just need to locate places where I can find a particular kind of soil, and a particular kind of rope—and I don't really want to recreate it all in my house, either—" He didn't want anyone inside his home anymore.

She looked thoughtful for a long moment. Finally, she said, "Well, I can't help you find rope or soil, but I do have a friend with an art gallery downtown. It's a little place. It could be perfect for an interview. It's totally empty, so I doubt she'd mind some light traffic."

"Oh? What's it called?"

"Downtown Heart." Rachel opened her purse and pulled out a tiny notebook—because she was the kind of woman who still wrote things down with a pen on paper—and scribbled something before tearing the leaf out and passing it to Dan.

"Here you go," she said. "Her name is Sapphire Gianni. I'm sure she'd be happy to help you out. She's not hosting any exhibits for another week or so. She just got back from vacation in Italy."

Dan cursed his memory, which swelled and colored with impressions of his and Annie's Italian backpacking honeymoon. Even as he hugged Rachel goodbye, he was mentally fighting to push Annie to arm's length. Some days, it felt as if she were still right beside him, trying to be heard. Felt. Seen. She flashed through his mind in cuffed jeans and a heather gray t-shirt, hair pulled back in a simple ponytail, pinching a white grape between two fingers, presenting it to him to try. It had been a humid afternoon; he remembered the light sweat on her neck and face. Her mouth moved and her eyes were bright with discovery, but that was all he could remember. Thank God.

In a dark way, he realized he was relieved this mysterious case had opened up at his feet. It was the first time since Annie's death that he had something to really care about again.

Downtown Heart was indeed a small place. A skinny brick structure sandwiched between two much larger shops—a consignment clothing store and a bicycle repair shop with vintage bikes on display in the window—so small Dan missed it the first time he passed, even though he was on foot.

He pushed the front door open, and it tinkled softly. Cool air-conditioned air embraced him with the competing aromas of lavender and dust. The walls were bare, the pedestals and cases empty, awaiting the art they would eventually feature.

"Is that Detective Winters?" a throaty female voice called down from a loft. "I'm coming right down. You're early!"

"Yes, I should have called," Dan said, shifting the black canvas backpack on his shoulder and squinting up into the recesses of the loft. He now could see it was accessible by a wooden ladder. How apropos.

A fleshy Mediterranean woman emerged from a dark alcove and began climbing gracefully down the ladder. Her wild mahogany hair hung loose, the kind of mane Dan imagined had never been touched by product, some of it naturally forming into snarls and curls. She wore a red tank top so tiny it might have been purchased in a kid's department, and a voluminous skirt of faded pink with a deep red hem. Jewelry weighed down her ankles and wrists. Bare feet. She couldn't have been older than thirty.

"Oh, it's fine," Sapphire reassured him. She was a thick woman, but not in a cumbersome way; she seemed almost weightless on her feet. "Did you want to talk to me or something? Rachel told me the interviews were of a very sensitive nature." As she crossed the gallery, Dan saw that all her features were strong: a hawkish nose, strong jaw, full lips, and eyes that were smoky and glittery at the same time. She reminded Dan of Eunice Boddington from the forensics lab: inner beauty and intelligence poured out of her, and she likely left a swath of infatuated men in her wake, wherever she traveled.

"I actually wanted to set something up before they got here," Dan explained, arching one shoulder to demonstrate that he had brought a backpack along. "Would you mind showing me the area you have planned for us?"

"Sure, sure. Right this way." Sapphire gestured toward a small table and two chairs at the back of the gallery. "Normally, there's a guest book here, but everything is still in storage. Until next week, anyway."

"Oh? And then what happens?" Dan said, mostly to be polite. He settled his backpack onto one of the chairs and opened it, placing three large platters in a circle at the center of the table.

"We've got our first artist of the new school year," Sapphire explained proudly. "She's pretty experimental." Her tone bordered on smug.

"Sounds interesting," Dan mumbled, removing a pouch of terra rossa soil from his backpack. He shook it loose onto the plate, not noticing Sapphire's frown.

"She does very grim dreamscapes. I'm hosting her series, Blood Red Lips."

"Mmm," Dan said, only half listening as he positioned the fruits and flowers around the plate.

"Lots of death imagery," Sapphire went on. "Lots of romanticism too, though. The canvases are very rich. Her favorite piece has lots of blood-filled wine glasses."

Gooseflesh broke out on Dan's arms at the words, and he hesitated as he placed the rope alongside the soil on the platter. "What?"

"I said there's a lot of blood in wine glasses in this one piece. Obviously, the artist is seeking to normalize death, to even romanticize it and let the Grim Reaper seduce us, but I find it heavy-handed." She rolled her eyes to the right. "Almost juvenile." To the other side. "And a little gross." She started to smile again. "But it's not bad, it's good. Just not my style. You should come see the show. I'm sure she'll sell lots of pieces, and the prices are fair since she's not yet known."

"Maybe," Dan said. He had to admit, the artist's obsession with death and wine made him curios. He wondered if she might have known Branden and Raymond. What if Amanda's obsession had been a new female friend, an exciting and dangerous artist type, rather than another man?

The soft tinkle of the swinging door drew Dan's attention away from his thoughts, and he saw that his first expert had arrived: Charlotte Hayes, an author and professor, a woman approaching seventy. She oozed sophistication, from the loosely knotted white and orange floral silk scarf around her throat, to the soft, beige leather of her gloves.

Her wide hips twitched from side to side and her small heels tapped a slow rhythm on the hardwood as she approached.

"Hello, all," Charlotte greeted them confidently.

Dan leaned forward and extended a hand. "Miss Hayes." She let him take her hand in a limp, oddly cupped position, and then stared down her nose at him, clearly waiting for something. Uncertain, Dan pecked her glove with his lips.

Apparently satisfied, she withdrew. "Detective Winters," she said, warm and cool at the same time.

Dan pulled out a chair for her but she declined with a barely perceptible shake of her head and a slight perfunctory smile.

"Thank you for meeting with me," Dan said. Sapphire took the cue to retreat to her loft.

Charlotte tilted her head back and forth thoughtfully as she approached the small table, where the three plates sat. She examined the plate of plums, cherries, eucalyptus leaves, and terra rossa. "I must say that I am …" her voice trailed off as she regarded the plate of chocolate and olives and pepper … "very intrigued as to the nature …" she said as she touched the handwoven rope on the Turner plate … "of your call," she finished flatly. She glanced up at Dan, stared for a second, then scoffed and said, "I don't have time for games, darling."

She turned on her heel to leave, but Dan sprang after her. "I won't waste your time, Miss Hayes."

She considered him from over her shoulder. "Being an expert can also make you a target for all manner of foolishness," she said tightly. "This isn't the strangest thing I've been invited to taste."

"Oh, no, you misunderstand. I don't want you to try these. I just want you to smell them." He hurried to take out a pad of paper for notes and explained as best he could.

She nodded and frowned, seeming both concerned and a little lost. "I appreciate that you've reached out to me for this, but there's nothing for me to tell you. If I may be so bold as to take your number, I will call you if anything comes to mind. I try to keep my wits sharp. You never know."

Dan scrawled down his number and tore the paper loose, passing it to her.

"I am going to pray for you, detective." She bowed slightly, turned, and departed.

When the bell dinged again, two sets of footsteps echoed through the space as Kristin approached with her mentor, Professor Irwin Kinsley. He was slim, tall, and bald, somewhere in his fifties, dressed in a cheerful royal blue cardigan and a red bowtie. Kristin, on the other hand, wore leather sandals and a loose dress in a vibrant emerald hue. It naturally contrasted with her golden skin.

"Hello, Dan," she said.

For a second, he felt as if he was the only person in the room. "Kris," he said, nodding to her. He didn't want to offer her his hand; it was all sweaty. Instead, he stretched his hand to the professor. "Professor Kinsley."

Kristin explained how Irwin had taught her everything she knew today.

"Maybe you'll be able to teach me something today as well," Dan said. He told the grim tale for the second time that day. It seemed all he ever did anymore was tell the story of the three murders, searching for the missing piece. It had been only a few weeks, but it felt like much longer.

When Dan was finished, Irwin regretfully informed him that he could see no connection between the Friulano, the Coonawarra, and the Syrah. "All three are the offspring of obscure grapes. The Friuli region is in the northeast of Italy, and the Rhône Valley wine comes from southeastern France. They're separated by hundreds of miles. The Coonawarra, of course, is Australian. They are all unique, and no, I don't see a common thread."

Again, Dan was forced to just exchange contact information and bid the man a good day. As Irwin passed through the door and back onto the street, Kristin turned to Dan and said, "We still have one left."

Dan nodded, though he was starting to feel hopeless. Maybe the killer was a genuine psychopath, and there was no method for predicting which wine would be the star of his next homage—or which San Franciscan.

The third interviewee Kristin had snagged for Dan, food critic Jack Stevens, was almost twenty minutes late. Dan had already packed up his plates and ingredients when the door swung open one more time and the same smart-looking, small-statured man from The Palace Hotel Restaurant three weeks earlier—the night of Branden Bullard's "jump"—strolled in casually as if he was right on time, with Kristin just behind him.

"Detective Dan," Jack beamed as he strode toward the table.

"Is that Jack Stevens I hear?" Sapphire called from the recesses of her alcove.

"Sapphire, my love!" he called out as she emerged from the shadows.

"Please tell me you're coming to the opening next week. There will be food here if you want to critique it!"

Jack laughed heartily. "I only care if there will be wine." He swung out a hand to be shaken by Dan. Jack Stevens had a dynamic energy percolating under his skin, which Dan did not. Although it was still early afternoon on a Saturday, Dan was already exhausted, but Jack looked ready to wrestle. He wore tailored khaki pants with a blue-and-white striped shirt, making his small frame less noticeable. Dan hadn't noticed because he'd been seated at the restaurant, but Jack Stevens was quite short, and he clearly dressed to compensate for it. *So he only seems confident,* Dan thought, *but he is self-conscious.* His graying hair was short and neat, and light gold glasses frames balanced on his slim nose.

"Kristin has told me so much about you," Jack said.

"Then I'm jealous," Dan said. "She never told me she knew Jack Stevens."

The other man simpered, enjoying the compliment. "You read my column?"

"Yes, I do. Your summer brunch series was transcendental."

Jack's eyes gleamed. "You thought so?"

"And how do you know Kristin?" Dan said, changing the subject from shamelessly fawning over the food critic.

"We were certified through the same institution. We met at an alumni banquet."

Kristin burst out laughing. "Almost certified, Jack," she reminded him, giving his arm a playful shove. Dan was surprised at the throb of jealousy that pulsed through him. "You were almost certified with me."

"That's true," Jack said, a note of chagrin in his voice. "I had to sidestep my way into a successful career involving fine wine." He winked at Kristin, and she beamed. "But no, the exam didn't go as well for me as it may have gone for you."

"Well, you're in good company. Dan failed his Master exam too." She patted Jack on the shoulder and Dan smiled at the other man, even though he felt as if he could fall right through the floor. He was surprised at how much a fumble from fifteen years past could still bother him.

"Oh? But you still work in wine as well?"

Dan found himself almost embarrassed to admit he was only a lowly detective. "I'm afraid that wasn't in the cards for me. I left behind my sommelier dreams in my mid-twenties, and now I'm working with the San Francisco Police Department on a few unsolved suicides that happened this month."

Jack nodded gravely, his demeanor chilling. "Unsolved suicides," he repeated.

"Actually, homicides."

"I see. And our skills—Kristin, the sommelier, and myself, the critic—how are those valuable to you, detective?"

"I'm developing a theory regarding the murders," Dan explained. "Each crime scene pays tribute to a specific wine, featuring its flavors, colors, and pairings. If I could just understand why the killer is selecting these wines and these people, perhaps I could anticipate his—or her—movements and end this psychopathy."

"That's admirable," Jack said. Dan knew what he was going to say next. "I just don't know how much help I'm going to be."

Dan patiently walked Jack through the sensorial input of each crime scene, the reviewer nodding, absorbing, and agreeing with Dan's conclusions. But when Dan asked Jack's opinion, he raised his eyebrows and shrugged.

"You know more than I do in this regard, I'm afraid."

"Well." Dan exhaled heavily. This entire project had been a bust. "Thank you for troubling to meet with me, anyway. I suppose it was still worth it, if only to be able to say now that I've met Jack Stevens of 'SF Cornucopia.'" The two of them shifted to exit the gallery. "You know," Dan added, "I—"

"Before you go—" Kristin cut in from slightly behind them.

Dan supposed he'd almost forgotten about her for a moment, but as soon as he looked back at her, he wondered how he could have. Her eyes were wide and hopeful, searching his with a girlish little smile. Something about her was different—her features all seemed to have an edge, a drama they normally lacked—and he realized she was wearing makeup. Had she always worn makeup?

"What if we all did something together instead?" she said. She didn't address Jack. Only Dan. "It's such a gorgeous day, and I don't have any plans. City's filled with parks and beaches. What do you think?"

"Hmm." Dan considered the idea. Going out on a sunny day with a beautiful woman and a new friend—a local celebrity, even—didn't seem like something he would do. He couldn't recall the last time he'd gone out into nature and been social with people. But he took a deep breath, and almost to his own surprise, the words flowed out of him. "That sounds wonderful."

"How about you, Jack?" Kristin called over Dan's shoulder, as if the other man's presence was only an afterthought. "Do you want to take this conversation to the park? It's a beautiful day."

"I think I could make time for that."

As the trio stepped toward the door, Dan bade goodbye and thanks to Sapphire, and Jack called out to her, "If I can't make it to the opening, Sapphire, just enjoy all the wine for me!" Grinning now, his bright blue eyes shifted to Dan. "So, detective, how did you fail your master somm exam, eh? Let's talk!"

Kristin snickered.

"It's the most challenging test in the world, you know," Dan reminded her, prickling.

"That's right." Jack patted his shoulder to reassure him. "You tell her."

"I know it's a difficult test," Kristin said. "I didn't pass it until my third try."

"My failed question was in the service portion of the exam," Dan confessed, deciding it was time to tell the tale. He pushed open the gallery's door and let his guests pass him into the dazzlingly bright day. The sunlight and fresh air began to awaken Dan's mind, and he realized he did feel like doing something today. Kristin was right. They couldn't waste it.

"It was silly," he went on. "I fumbled a question about aperitifs. I wanted to go back and retest, but—" He remembered why he had not returned the next year to retake the service portion of the exam. He'd met Annie.

Annie had always known she would get cancer. It was in her genes, and it had been identified by the presence of JAK2 in her DNA years before her health began to deteriorate. She had been in her residency, studying to be an oncologist, when they found each other. She wasn't yet sick then. She and Dan fell into a groove with alarming speed, as if their second date had been a wedding, and he forgot about the master sommelier exam. They moved in together and her concerns became his. Taking the exam again would cost another thousand dollars. He would have to travel a great distance to take it. In any case, that option seemed leagues away from him by then. He had fallen in love with a doomed heroine. His dream to become a sommelier had faded. Annie became his dream.

As they reached the corner of the bicycle repair shop, Dan realized that Jack and Kristin were gazing at him expectantly. He remembered he'd been in the middle of a sentence when Annie had cropped up in his mind.

"—but" he repeated, continuing as if this lapse hadn't happened, "life got in the way."

His phone vibrated in his pocket, and he extracted it, secretly thankful for the break from Jack and Kristin's scrutiny, as nice as they both were. They idled and made quiet chit-chat as he turned his attention to the call. "Chief?"

"Magic Man," Chief boomed across the line. "What would you say if I offered you the opportunity to come in to work on a beautiful Saturday afternoon?"

"I would say that this is the first Saturday in a thousand Saturdays that I've truly wanted to do what I'm doing right now, Chief."

"Ahhh, that's a shame! That is a shame. Here's the problem. We've got another body at Half Moon Bay, and I want you to take a look at it."

"Oh?" Dan turned from Kristin and Jack and lowered his voice further. "A suicide, or—?"

"It looks like a suicide," Chief said, "but it's weird. It's weird. You know what I mean. Turner was weird. Vasquez was weird. This is weird. You'll see what I mean when you get down here."

Dan cast a glance over his shoulder at Jack and Kristin. Kristin laughed at something Jack said, then her eyes flicked to Dan as if checking to see whether he'd heard it. Dan quickly looked away.

"You'll want to see this," Chief went on. "Even more than you want to do whatever it is you were about to do."

Dan shook his head, but the shake evolved into a nod, and he told Chief okay and ended the call.

As he looked back at Kristin and Jack, her gaze softened, interpreting what he was about to say before he could say it. "You can't come with us."

"That's right. Work. I've got to go."

Jack tsked. "It was a pleasure to meet you, sir. May we meet again." He gave Dan a brisk handshake before turning to Kristin and extending an arm for her. "And you, my dear. Shall we? To the park?"

Kristin pulled her eyes from Dan and nodded, sliding her arm through Jack's and letting him tug her along the sidewalk. She smiled at Dan from over her shoulder before joining Jack's pace.

It seemed to Dan that her eyes did not look particularly wistful, but he told himself not to read into it and waved goodbye to her. He took some tiny, bitter consolation in the fact that walking alongside Kristin made Jack look very small.

7

ON THE LEES

Although the weather throughout San Francisco seemed to be balmy and mild all over, a strong, salty breeze peeled off the Pacific Ocean at Half Moon Bay beach. Towering dunes flanked the space behind Dan, creating an intense atmosphere: the high and the low, the wind and the water, all roiling together.

The smells swelling around him were incredible: saline, oysters, wet stones slapping with rolling foam. A distant fragrance floated on the air like a bottle of spilled perfume in another room—citrus and peach again. It felt like Dan's blood chilled in his veins as he stepped under the caution tape that cordoned off the entire beach. He passed Barry North with a nod, which North Star returned with his cruller in mock salute. A clot of officers at the shoreline drew Dan toward the narrow ribbon of wet sand.

At first, he couldn't see it. He couldn't smell the decay yet either, but he knew the body was still here. He didn't know how he knew, maybe because everyone was focused on one spot. It wouldn't be long before the corpse would be taken away, though. He must have been early to the scene this time, because in drowning cases the body would be on its way to forensics posthaste.

Dan broke through the hedge of murmuring analysts and saw Chief kneeling over a grayish, splotchy, swollen young man. His hair was still dark with wetness, flecked with sand and garlanded with seaweed. The skin on his hands and feet had puckered deeply, and his gray lips had cracked and peeled in the California sunshine. He wore nothing but waterlogged white underwear, and thin cuts laced his body as if he'd been dragged over fine rocks. His features were lost to the process of bloating, so his chin and his jawline were vague, and Dan could only imagine what he'd looked like in life. All he could ascertain for sure was that this man had been relatively young and Caucasian.

Nearby was a sand-caked, faded blue towel, mangled as if from a hard struggle. Divots gouged into the sand at the base of the towel immediately told Dan that someone, at some point, had been pounding their feet into the earth. Clothes rested in a sloppy pile at the side of the towel. A garishly striped tin of hard candies lay nearby, open and melting in the sun. Small, torn-open, red plastic packages littered a halo around the towel. There was a pan of exposed bread, ruined by seagulls now. A water-damaged book lay open, its rippled pages fluttering back and forth in the breeze. A half-eaten peach rested next to the towel, crusted with sand and fringed with coils of orange rind.

Dan swallowed. He saw what Chief had meant. It was weird. It was the same weirdness again, just different.

"Sean Mugneret," Chief said, introducing the corpse to Dan.

Mugneret. Another victim of French descent.

"He appears to have drowned in the bay. He washed up in front of some sunbathers."

Dan stepped closer to the deceased, leaning down to look with Chief. All the victims were so young. This man looked no older than thirty. His skin had a grayish tint, but it hadn't yet turned greenish bronze and become pimpled. A corpse submerged for more than forty-eight hours would develop pimples and lose its skin, essentially becoming soap in the water. But this epidermis looked sturdy, meaning the death almost certainly occurred the previous night.

"What else do we know about him?" Dan asked. He wondered if the victim was friends with the others.

"He was thirty-two and lived in Napa Valley, where he ran a winery called Family Grove."

A winery. Dan was not surprised in the least. "Any new friends?"

"Christ, Winters, we haven't even got the body to the lab yet," Chief snapped. "Speak of the devil."

An ambulance bleeped in the parking lot, its lights silently whirling. Dan stepped to the other side to give the EMTs space, and Chief followed.

"So …" Chief said, nodding slowly. His gaze shifted to Dan. He seemed to want to say something but was unable to get it out. Finally, he blurted, "So, Magic Man, what do you think?" He bulged his eyes at Dan. "Does this tripe fit your theory or not?"

Dan slid his hands into gloves and looked first at the damaged novel. It was a compilation text: *Voyages extraordinaires* by Jules Verne.

Dan grimaced. Like the handwoven rope and the fresh paint, this would be the detail he would not understand until it was too late.

"I don't know anything about Jules Verne," he confessed. The tin of candies said Rigolettes on it. Dan sighed. It had been a long time since his days of furiously studying for the sommelier exam; what was he missing here? He examined the torn plastic: LU La Coqueline cookies, uneaten. Chocolatey, buttery madeleines. Why all these decadent sweets, uneaten? The tin of bread was unevenly torn, an obvious feast for seagulls.

"I don't know," he said again. "I don't see the connection between all these foods and any wine."

He closed his eyes and inhaled, savoring the saltiness in the air. Was that a piece of the puzzle, or a coincidence? Was this a simple drowning, a candy junkie, a fan of classic French literature, and nothing more? The flat expression of disapproval on Chief's face said yes. He had evidently hoped for more from his magician, and Dan wasn't delivering.

"But Sean Mugneret is French," Dan said, trying to rescue his floundering theory. "And he owned a winery."

"That's not enough, Winters," Chief barked. "You can't connect these victims through their ethnicity, and you can't connect them through their occupations. Turner was a DJ. Bullard was a student. Vasquez was a goddamn coder. They knew each other. Connection. But there's no reason to assume Mugneret knew any of the other victims. He's older. He's more commercially successful. He didn't even live in this area. There are no connections between this victim and the others. I would say they're not related at all, but then there's the scene here," he allowed. "Something ain't right. It's the same, but not." He scowled at the foods in the sand. "Why are these kids dressing their suicides up like a game?"

Dan knew there was more here than they were seeing, especially Chief. This was the same killer he had been seeking everywhere, the same killer who knew he was watching, knew he was in pursuit. Dan scanned the sandy cliffs at their backs, but he saw no one up there.

Dan spent his Sunday researching the life of Sean Mugneret. He found the man's birthdate, when he applied for his business license, and when his passport was last stamped, but he couldn't get his nose in the case the way he wanted to. Without something more to hook onto, it would have to be closed as a suicide, even though Mugneret had none of the markers of a suicidal individual.

Monday morning, he gave in and called Family Grove, hoping for some answers. He got the answering machine and was on the verge of leaving a brief message when a clearing throat behind startled him into dropping his phone.

"Winters," Chief said from behind him. He didn't call him Magic Man when he was displeased. "There's something I have to tell you, and I want you to relax and shut the hell up when I say it. Follow me."

Dan followed, unsure what he had done this time. He couldn't remember breaking any rules recently—except just a few seconds ago, calling the Family Grove winery behind Chief's back.

When they passed into Chief's office, the big man closed the door and locked it. "Forensics got back to us with a murder weapon."

"A murder weapon?" This was a break from the formula. What did it mean? "What was it? Where was it?"

"It washed up on the beach yesterday, and a jogger turned it in, knowing what had happened on the beach Saturday. It's called a dodine."

The back of Dan's neck prickled with recognition. He knew what a dodine was, and the look on Chief's face said he did too.

"A wine stirrer," Chief grumbled.

A dodine was an instrument of curious appearance—a thin, curved metal rod with a blunt grip on one end and a freely rotating blade used to stir lees, the sediment in barrels of wine. The blade must have caused all the cuts, while the grip caused the bruises.

"For battonage," Dan said. "I knew it. I KNEW IT!"

Chief's eyes were flat with disapproval again. Why? Dan had brought him a solid theory, hadn't he?

"Yes, it does appear that this death is a murder, and that it is somehow linked to wine." His voice soured as it rolled over the word "wine" as if he was talking about a ridiculous fad and not a custom that originated no later than the fourth century BC. It's basically the oldest recorded beverage, aside from water.

Chief was still unaccountably sour as he said, "Since you know so much about this stuff, I'm placing you as a primary investigator for all four cases. The connection is obvious now, even if it's not obvious to me—or to you, Magic Man. There's still a lot of work here to be done."

"Yes, sir," Dan agreed. "Could the lab get any info about the foods around the towel? Or the book? Anything?"

"That big biscuit was some brioche-type thing. Rum. Oranges. I forget what they called it, but it's in the file now."

Dan nodded, thinking.

"To me," Chief ventured, his voice softening as if he was speaking to a partner and not an underling, "it seems that Mugneret went to meet a friend. The meeting turned ugly somehow. Those other bodies didn't have any marks on them, but Mugneret's did. The other suicides actually killed themselves, or at least, were found in positions where it's possible—or probable—that they did it to themselves. But not Mugneret."

"Maybe that's why it turned ugly."

"Maybe," Chief said.

It was Wednesday night and Dan had been over it a hundred times now. His home library was overrun with papers. Turner, Bullard, Vasquez, Mugneret. Aged twenty-eight, twenty-four, thirty-three, and thirty-two. Two with known French ancestry. Three friends. San Francisco and Napa. Friulano, Coonawarra, Syrah, and now, a fourth, unknown wine. Who connected them? How? Why were they chosen? He rubbed his temples. He paced across the room. He grew hungry but didn't have the will to pull himself away from the study.

Finally, his phone vibrating on his desk brought his focus to something small and manageable, and he was relieved for the opportunity to have a simple challenge: just answer the phone.

His head lightened instantly, and the ghost of a smile crossed his lips. He saw the name on the screen and answered the call.

"Hey, it's Kristin."

"I know. How are you doing?"

"I'm good." She sounded as if she meant it. "I got off work early today, and I invited a friend to join me at Bacchus, but she can't make it. Sooo ... I was wondering if maybe you might want to come with me?"

Dan glanced at his papered desk, then tore his eyes away from it. He did need to get away. Get some space. Get out of here. "That sounds fantastic. What time?"

"Oh! Um, how about eight o'clock?"

"I'll be there."

He wondered what time it was. It felt like seven; he would need to jump in the shower right away. He felt the strange urge to change his clothes before going out. He wondered what colors would look best on him. Did he have anything modern, hip? He didn't think so. But he would look. He'd find something.

He arrived shortly before eight, certain Kristin would be late. "Table for two," he said, fussing with his black silk tie to ensure it was resting smoothly on his black dress shirt. Was it too much? He wore gray slacks and a matching suit jacket. He'd get the table, look at the menu, tell himself he wasn't nervous, and intentionally not check the freshness of his breath—

"Actually," the host said, "I believe your date may already be here."

"Oh, she's not—it's not a date—"

"If you say so," the host simpered, gesturing into the wine bar.

Dan followed his direction and saw Kristin waving at him from a table in the back. He blushed as he realized she'd probably been watching him adjust his tie and smooth his lapels.

Her long copper hair was gathered into a thick, artfully mussed braid down one shoulder, and she looked both elegant and modest in a casual black maxi dress and sandals. Again, the detail of her makeup caught his attention. Tonight, she had bold cherry lips. He'd never seen her look so … sexy. *Is she purposely trying to look like that? For me?*

"Hey, Kris."

She sprang from her seat and wrapped her arms around his neck, pressing her body close for a brief but intense hug. Her skin swam in the scent of vanilla and cinnamon, probably from some kind of lotion or shampoo. Whatever it was, it made him want to curl up inside the curve of her neck and fall asleep.

"Daniel," she said, exhaling softly before settling back into her seat. "How are you doing? I saw you Saturday, but it feels like forever." Before they could truly settle in and catch up with the happenings of the past four days, a waiter arrived, and they ordered their first glasses. As they waited for their drinks, Kristin leaned across the little table wedged between them, her eyes bright with conspiratorial electricity. "So," she whispered, "what's going on with your cases?"

Dan related the scene at Half Moon Bay, as much as he could divulge, and Kristin listened intently. "I don't know," he concluded in frustration. "I don't see the common thread in this one."

Kristin sniffed the air. "What about your nose? It was the best in our class."

He grimaced and closed his eyes, recalling the scene. "I just don't know. Strangely, the scent was—clotted. All I could smell was the salt in the air. It was the damn beach. He was floating in the water. All kinds of evidence probably washed away."

"Hmm. But what if it wasn't? What if the salt and the ocean were part of the palate all along?"

Their waiter arrived with the wine, poised to pour into Kristin's glass, but she fanned out her palm to him suddenly. "Actually, hold it," she commanded. "Can you bring me a … a Muscadet instead, please?"

The waiter frowned, but said, "Of course."

Dan watched Kristin, and it suddenly reminded him of Annie. He used to love watching her mind work, too.

"What are you thinking, Kris?"

"The salinity," she almost whispered. "The high salinity reminds me of—of Nantes, full of marshes and high-mineral soil. The melon de Bourgogne white grape tastes almost like—like oyster. And it's fermented on the lees, and stirred with—"

"—a dodine," they said in unison.

The waiter returned with a bottle of Muscadet, pouring the creamy, almost pure green wine into Kristin's glass. As she swirled it, she closed her eyes and inhaled deeply, savoring its aroma. Dan couldn't help but admire her beauty in the moment, and it wasn't a matter of her physique or facial features. It was about how she lost herself in her senses, just as Dan often did.

Then her eyes snapped open, and she extended her glass to him. "Try it. Tell me that isn't right."

Dan took the glass from her, swirled, and sniffed, even though he already knew she would be right. He closed his eyes and could already see the shore again.

"The treats on the beach make sense too. I can't believe I missed it." Kristin's voice floated to him in the darkness. "They're all references to Nantes. The cookies. The candies. The bread. It was … it was *fouace nantaise*! It's all food from Nantes. Oh!" she yelped, clapping excitedly. "The book—Jules Verne! He was from Nantes!"

Dan opened his eyes and whispered, "Coonawarra Cabernet Sauvignon. Northern Rhône Syrah. Friulano. Muscadet. What's the connection?"

They savored the entire bottle, mulling over the details together. Dan's lips loosened and he forgot completely about confidentiality. He poured out every thought that had entered his brain over the past few weeks. With his face resting in the palm of his hand and his eyes drifting sleepily around the wine bar, he felt as comfortable as he would be in his own home. He told Kristin everything about the victims, everything about how he felt consumed, obsessed. How, despite the grudging faith Chief had finally placed in him, he still felt alone. The only detail he kept from her was the box of wines on his stoop. He didn't want to scare her. He just wanted to get this weight off his shoulders. He needed a woman with a keen ear and a strong and sympathetic mind to listen to him ramble.

"You're going to catch this psycho," Kristin promised him, stretching her arm across the table, and covering his hand with hers. "Let's get out of here. It's stuffy."

"You think so?"

"Yeah. A little fresh air would do us both good."

Dan almost didn't want this night to be perfect. Maybe it was just the Muscadet in his system, but everything seemed to be brushed with a euphoric sheen, and Kristin seemed to see it too. Her eyes were starry, and her mouth wore a constant smile. They strode beneath streetlamps until they could access North Beach from the road. Kristin slid off her sandals and hitched up her voluminous dress. Dan stuck his hands in his pockets and kept his eyes on the dark, roiling sea beyond them. Kristin was too pretty right now; he didn't want to look at her. It was easier to gaze across the infinite, peaceful shadow of the ocean, to listen to the waves and watch the silhouettes of ships in the deep distance.

"This is better." Kristin breathed softly, staring out across the horizon with him. "Much better."

Dan forced himself to look over at her and was startled to see that she'd stripped her hair of its elastic bands and was now threading her fingers through the braid, unraveling her hair until it began to move in the breeze.

"Yeah, it is."

Kristin gave him a pensive look. "Do you feel like you might be working yourself too hard?"

He considered her question and shook his head. "I need it," he assured her. "It fills my head up when nothing else will."

She went on hesitantly. "It's just all so dark. It seems like filling your head up with darkness is … is bound to cause you pain."

Dan didn't say what he was thinking. His head was filled with darkness most of the time now. There was nothing anyone could do about that, not even bright-eyed Kristin.

"Ever since Annie—" He stopped himself and breathed, shaking his head. "It's like I've been trying to solve her suicide, too."

Kristin stiffened but said nothing. Dan felt her hovering next to him, watching him. He could smell her perfume enveloping him.

"It was just like Amanda Turner, really. All the pieces were in place to call it a suicide—a classic, open-and-shut case. And yet, I just can't see it. I knew Annie, you know?" He paused, then added, "That was what Amanda Turner's ex-boyfriend told me that made me look deeper into her case in the first place. He said that he knew her, and she would never do a thing like that. And I knew what he meant. That's exactly how I felt about Annie."

He stared at Kristin for just a beat or two too long, then felt uncomfortable and shifted his gaze back to the sea. "I've had too much to drink," he announced with false cheer. "I'm sorry."

He was expecting the usual Kristin behavior—a giggle, a reassuring smile, a pat on the shoulder. But she wasn't doing any of those things. She was watching him closely and nodding with a sudden sobriety he didn't think he'd ever seen in her.

"You don't have to be sorry. You should talk about her to somebody. You need to get these feelings out."

Dan felt a small, sad smile kinking the corner of his lip. "Maybe. But I'm guessing that somebody shouldn't be you."

Kristin squinted at him with confusion. The breeze tussled her hair, and she looked like a perfume ad in a magazine with the full moon behind her and her lips as dark and juicy as berries.

"What do you mean?" she asked, coming half a step closer. That extra half-step was a crucial measurement of space, and Dan tensed. The only thing between them was a narrow strip of emptiness. He could feel the tips of her hair flicking against his shirt, they stood so close.

"Why not me? Am I not your friend?" Her neck lolled aside, and her heavy eyelashes trembled. She radiated receptivity.

"Of course, you're my—my friend." Something was happening without Dan's permission: the air between them grew warmer and pulsated with potential energy. She closed her eyes.

Dan went cold all over. What was he supposed to do? Say "Excuse me"? Call her name to rouse her from this pre-kiss trance?

His cheeks burned, he cleared his throat, and all the words came spilling out of his mouth. "Kristin, I—I'm sorry if I gave you the wrong impression—" Her eyes flew open as though he had told her there were snakes on the ground. "And you do look very pretty tonight, so pretty, a man can't think—"

"I'm the one who's sorry, Dan, sorry, I don't know what I was thinking, of course, of course—" Her mortification came across just as loudly as her other emotions always did. "I—you—I thought this was a date," she said softly. "I'm so sorry, Daniel. I feel like an idiot."

Her eyes dimmed. Dan winced to see it happen and know that he had caused that dampness to pass over her light.

"It was just … the moon," he said in a sudden, desperate grab for something to alleviate the awkwardness of the moment. "Look at it up there. And this gorgeous ocean doesn't help. And the bottle of Muscadet, Kris. It was the bottle of Muscadet. Don't apologize. Anyone would have tried to kiss me."

Kristin laughed, and Dan was grateful for the sound.

He stared at himself in the bathroom mirror as he brushed his teeth. He couldn't help but wonder if the killer had watched him do that to Kristin. He had totally humiliated her. He shook his head at his reflection. How could he, with his sad, puffy eyes and his five o'clock shadow, be attractive to a woman like her? He didn't get it.

He collapsed into bed and plunged through the darkness, to the place beyond. The mist. The nonsense commands. Alarms and childhood rhymes and words that that weren't even words … and then the haze cleared, and he was home again. He had passed through the mists of nonsense unscathed. He entered the living room, and time slowed to a stop. The world around him stretched and shrank, again and again, all around the focal part of Annabelle Winters's dead body.

She lay sprawled across the carpet right beside the couch, as if she'd fallen, and she was already the color of ash. Her eyes weren't frozen open yet, but that would happen after another hour or two. She still looked alive, in some ways, but he knew she wasn't. He knew it.

His feet dragged as he crossed the floor and lowered himself. He bowed lower and lower until his face was pressed into the carpet, and he moaned, "Tell me the truth, Annie," digging his fingers into its fibers. His hands clenched into fists, and he tore the rug off the floor, flinging it behind him mercilessly. His breath came in gushes, and he heard thunder overhead. The carpet eroded into mud and Dan's eyes flew up to where Annie's body had just been.

He was in the cemetery now.

He kneeled at her grave with muddy hands. Two deep gashes were gouged into the earth in front of him. He took a deep breath and settled himself.

"Was it really the medicine?" he whispered. Thunder cracked above him. "Where did you go in those last weeks?"

His heart began to vibrate, which was odd. He put his hand inside his shirt and dug out a quivering sliver of light. He knew—somehow, he knew—it was Annie.

She was with him. Inside him.

But his heart was still vibrating.

He looked down and saw that his chest had become a gaping, growing hole. Some of Annie's magic fed into it—he could see how the edges of his wound sparkled—but for the most part it looked as if she was killing him from the inside out.

He awoke calling her name into the pillow. His chest was still vibrating, and he reared up grumpily, feeling the drool on his chin. He patted himself down and removed his cell phone from his front pocket. He'd fallen asleep fully clothed. Wearing shoes. He furrowed his brow at the phone's glowing faceplate. The number was Unknown.

Swiping his finger over the green icon, he brought the phone to his face. "Hello?"

"I'm so sorry, detective." Dan thought he recognized the pleasant, lightly accented female voice, and allowed the face to slowly materialize from his memory: Charlotte Hayes, the author and his first guest expert from the failed experiment at the gallery. "Were you sleeping?"

"Well, it's four o'clock in the morning, so yeah."

"I'm so sorry. I was back and forth about whether to call. It took this glorious bottle of Saar Riesling Auslese to convince me."

"Did something happen, Miss Hayes?" He had no patience right now. She had just woken him from a hellish nightmare, and he could still feel it clinging to his skin.

"I heard Sean Mugneret met an untimely end in recent days," Charlotte said. "He was something of a golden boy in Napa Valley, you know."

"I'm aware he had a winery there, yes."

"It's not just that. Sean was heir to grape gold, *mon ami*. He was a descendant of the Mongeard-Mugneret family."

"Right," Dan said. It had been so long since he'd memorized all the different villages and strains of grapes that the name meant nothing to him. "And that is a big deal?"

He heard her expel her breath in unveiled disgust. "Mongeard-Mugneret is a top Burgundy producer, Detective Winters. This is your case. Don't you want to solve it? If so, then educate yourself."

Dan politely ended the call with Charlotte Hayes, who he suspected to be a little drunk. He would fact-check her in the morning. Well, in the late morning.

Dan lay awake staring at the ceiling, lost in thought. Even if Sean Mugneret was heir to an important vineyard in France, that didn't necessarily connect him any more thoroughly to the other three victims. But it did have the makings of a solid motive, and that was what Chief needed from him right now. Answers. Any answers at all.

8

STORMY NIGHT

The sun was hidden behind a sheet of billowing gray that Monday morning. By the time Barry North's car reached Napa Valley, its muggy intensity would be pounding directly onto the roof. The wind was high and it smelled of soil and rain. At least traffic was light and moving swiftly. Dan watched the scenery roll by in the passenger's seat, enjoying the tiny feeling of relief that came from following Chief Brigham's orders.

Yes, Chief had been the one to command Dan and Barry to travel the hour and a half from San Francisco up to Napa, as if he now believed in his wayward detective. Of course, he hadn't needed to tack Barry North onto the assignment. But Barry North was notoriously boring and mild. He always did what he was supposed to do, and his life story was filled with practical decision making—not the sort of thing Dan was up to talking about the whole drive to Napa. Especially if, God forbid, Barry tried to make small talk.

But then again, he supposed having mind-numbing small talk on the ride would be okay. At least it would keep his mind off Kristin. Why had she tried to kiss him on the beach the other night? Couldn't she see that he was ... out of order?

"This can't be the place," Barry muttered, flicking his turn signal and curving with the road.

The sign read FAMILY GROVE WINERY, but Dan was struck by how much the palatial stone building at the end of the drive didn't seem to fit the victim. He was only in his early thirties when he died; how did he have this much property?

"Is this really the place?" Barry asked.

The car slowly crested the drive and pulled into one of many vacant spots. Monday morning wasn't exactly the hottest time to visit a winery. Barry put the car in park, looking befuddled as he climbed out and scowled at the structure. Dan was also confused as he exited the car. But upon closer inspection, a bronze plaque on the wraparound porch assured them that, yes, this was Sean Mugneret's Family Grove Winery. They ambled up the polished stairs and entered through the front door.

In keeping with the traditional exterior, the interior was a sweeping space paneled in polished cherrywood with a long counter in the center of the room. Bottles of wine lined the bar like decorations, and huge barrels lined the walls.

Dan heard the distinct tap of approaching footfalls, and then a professionally dressed black woman crossed through a door and onto the floor. Her voluminous coils were wrapped at the top of her head with a bright yellow headscarf, but the rest of her ensemble was monotone: black slacks and a black dress shirt tucked in.

"Welcome to Family Grove Winery," she said, bowing to both of them separately. "My name is Tania, and I'll be taking care of you today. Just the two of you?"

Dan and Barry exchanged a look, and Dan extended his badge for Tania, taking the lead.

"We're detectives with San Francisco PD," Dan explained, "and we're here to ask a few questions about the owner, Mr. Mugneret."

Tania's face drained of all its warmth and hospitality. She blinked. "Of course. I'm just the manager on duty, but I'd be happy to answer any questions you might have."

"If you're the manager on duty, you can probably tell us: who is running the winery now?"

"The investors," Tania said curtly. "Sean's family. They—they want us all to keep coming in while they sort out the paperwork and figure out how to keep this winery in their family."

"Got it," Dan said, offering her one of the seats at the bar. "Let's all sit and just talk."

He wasn't surprised that the first minute or two of the conversation consisted solely of Tania heartily emphasizing that she had no idea who might have been behind the murder. Dan decided to move onto something less threatening. Tania was obviously nervous. No one liked to be questioned by the police.

"Can you tell me what Mr. Mugneret has been like for the past few weeks? In general?"

She considered the question for several seconds, letting her head fall to one side. "Preoccupied," she said. "But also kind of excited. Sean already had that personality type—spontaneous, fickle—but there was more to it this time."

"Oh?" Dan took a guess. "Like maybe a new relationship?"

Tania's mouth soured. "If it was, he kept it to himself—but no. That's not what I mean. I didn't know too much about it, but he told me he'd made a connection with another member of wine royalty. They were seeing each other regularly, but the person never came to the winery with him. They were probably talking about going into business together. Sean was a businessman, first and foremost."

"Uh-huh. I see." But he wasn't sure he did see. Why would a new business partner—someone with whom there was likely no contract yet—want Sean Mugneret dead? What about his family members? They seemed eager enough to parcel off this little piece of Napa Valley that Sean had carved out for himself.

"Who exactly is giving the staff its orders as of right now?"

"Right now, Sean's father video conferences with the closing manager every night. But he wasn't the only investor. Mr. Mugneret took hundreds of thousands of dollars in investments from his extended family, the Mongeard-Mugnerets. They're all so obsessed with each other. They call it 'community,' but it's practically incest."

"Who is 'they'?"

"All the heirs to the area in Burgundy Sean was from—their domaine. He was a pretty level-headed man, but you could also tell that he thought he was something special, coming from family name in a region like Burgundy."

Dan's eyebrows rose. He looked to Barry to see if he was hearing what Dan was hearing, but no particular expression registered in the officer's eyes. He hadn't been following this case—these cases—closely like Dan had, so he didn't know this wasn't the first time someone who knew the victim had expressed bitterness at the exclusive nature of the victim's clique. Jermaine too had made a comment about how Amanda seemed to have become pretentious, and he blamed a circle of "family friends," a group to which he'd never been privy.

Dan wondered if it was the same group. Could Amanda have been "wine royalty"?

He couldn't imagine it. She seemed to have come from a coarse lifestyle and Turner was not a French surname. He remembered Branden Bullard's mother on the red asphalt at Eden Hope playground: Patricia Camuzet. *"He would only speak in French. My family is from France, but I don't even speak French these days ... He mocked me for mispronouncing something, and even ... even said it was a shame that I'd abandoned our culture."* But Amanda? Yet Jermaine had said the same thing. She had changed. Could Raymond and Amanda have been included in some rich French experience, even if it wasn't a part of their cultural heritage?

A small group of customers arrived, giddy in anticipation of their wine-tasting, so Dan and Barry thanked Tania for her time and left their contact information in case anything else came across her path.

"Well, darn," Barry said, climbing into the driver's seat of his car. "I don't know how useful any of that is going to be. It sounds like he might have been killed for his winery, but why would someone from France kill a guy in Napa? Especially when they're already rich and they've got stakes in the place as it is."

"I agree," Dan said, though his thoughts didn't end there. He knew this interview with Tania had value. There were spilled puzzle pieces in front of him; he just needed to put them all in the right place. It wasn't just murder, and it wasn't just wine. There was more here. He just couldn't yet pinpoint what it was.

Barry flicked his turn signal to return to the interstate, but Dan cleared his throat and hurried to say, "What if we hang out here a little longer?"

Barry frowned and considered, letting his car slow as it approached the junction. "Chief Brigham only told us to check out the winery."

"I know. But what are we bringing back to him, really? You said it yourself—that interview was a bust." Dan didn't believe that, but he wasn't above using someone else's misconceptions against them if it meant solving this case. "We're already here. Let's go get the keys to Mugneret's house."

Barry's frown deepened and he tapped his brakes, returning to the parking lot. He popped the car into park and stared at Dan. All around them, a heavy wind roiled and nudged the car back and forth on its wheels. Still, the pregnant cloud overhead wouldn't give up its water yet. "You have a reputation, you know," Barry said. "You don't heed authority. You get crackpot ideas. That's why you're stuck working suicide squad."

Dan grimaced. "I have my reasons. And I work suicide by choice."

"That's what you think."

"That's what I know." Dan's voice carried a hard edge with it, telling Barry to back off, and the other man quelled at his tone. "You have a reputation too, North Star, and that's why it's your ass that's here with me right now, not Manozza's. You're here because you're dutiful, even when Chief is wrong. You're here to babysit me."

"Because this is what you do! You go off on your own, you develop the case alone. It's dangerous, Winters. It's dangerous to you, and it's dangerous to your colleagues—and loved ones!"

A memory of Dan's nightmare—the ashen body sprawled in the living room, Annie seeming to be asleep, but so very pale—flashed through his mind and he blinked it away. The car rocked again with a sudden gale. It was going to storm hard, and soon.

"I'm not so clumsy that I hurt myself," Dan argued. "There's never been a time that I was forced into a sabbatical, never been a time that I saw myself demoted. Never visited a hospital bed that was caused by my decisions on a case. I'm going to keep someone out of the hospital, or the morgue, because I'm going to solve this case before the killer strikes again. That's the difference between us. I'm not trying to save myself. I'm trying to stop a killer. And I'll bring the evidence back to Chief alone if I have to. You want me to take the blame for solving this case against Chief's orders? I'll take it. It's worth it."

Barry turned away and settled into his seat again, thinking. Several seconds passed. "No," he finally said. He cranked the car up and pulled out of the parking space.

Dan glowered at North as he accelerated. Was the other detective forcing him to jump out of a car going sixty miles an hour to stay in Napa?

But when Barry exited the parking lot, he turned away from the interstate and glanced at Dan. "So, what's Mugneret's address? I know you already know it by heart."

"It's a chic little penthouse not far from here. I've seen the blueprints."

Barry blinked at him in surprise.

"The apartment complex managers are less than loyal," Dan said. "I emailed them this morning. The superintendent is expecting us."

Sean's apartment turned out to be spotless and well organized, which made locating any potential evidence easy. In a pile of mail on the granite kitchen countertop, Dan found a simple handwritten letter. The paper was coarse and creamy white, with some familiar filigree around the corners. He flipped the folded sides open and grimaced: the message inside was handwritten in spiky black pen. He knew this style.

"Bon appétit."

He couldn't find an envelope for it. If it was part of the mail pile, it had been slipped into the box without the aid of the post office. Wasn't this exactly the same message he had received? So, Sean had gotten it too—perhaps even the evening of his death. It wasn't as if anyone had brought in the mail since then.

Dan placed the note in an envelope for evidence. Just then, he heard the light, wet smack of rain droplets on Mugneret's apartment windows. The storm was settling in.

By the time Dan arrived home from the station, the sky was a mottled gray, the color of pigeon feathers, as hard, fat blasts of rain came in rounds lasting several minutes apiece. The wind never stopped. It howled menacingly and the walls groaned in response. He was wondering what he would do with his Monday night when he felt a soft rumbling in his pocket and pulled out his cell phone. It was Kristin.

Dan brought the phone to his ear. "Hey, Kristin," he said, trying to keep his voice casual. "What's up?"

"What's up? Look at you, Mr. So Discreet." Something was weird about her voice. It was almost a purr. "I just wanted to call and say thank you for your gift. I ... it wasn't expected, but it's definitely ... appreciated."

"I'm sorry, Kris, I'm not sure what you're talking about."

There was a pause on the line. "The wine you sent me." Another beat. "The Riesling?"

Dan's mouth moved, but no sound came out.

"With the note?" She sounded hesitant now.

"What note? Did this just happen?" Without thinking about it, Dan was already marching toward his front door, scowling as he whipped a gray windbreaker from his coatrack.

"Um, okay." All the happiness had drained from Kristin's voice. "I guess you did not send me this wine." She laughed uncomfortably, and Dan felt a pang at having caused her this embarrassment. "It's a bottle of Ürziger Würzgarten Riesling. It came with a sweet little note and some flowers. The note said, 'This bouquet reminds me of yours, if I were to swirl you in a glass.' Which I thought was weird because I do not smell like a Riesling. At least I don't think of myself like that."

Dan could hear his heartbeat in his ears. "Listen, Kris. There's something I have to tell you. The killer sent me some bottles of wine a few weeks ago. And I ... I did not send you any bottle of wine."

"Huh."

More silence. Dan felt her unease, and he was sure she knew that, and he hated it.

Another light, nervous laugh trickled over the line. "I suddenly feel like I'm not alone in this house anymore."

Dan winced. "I knew that he or she had been watching me. It's no small leap to imagine they would have seen you and could have begun to follow you as well. We never should have gone out the other night. Now they think

—" He didn't want to finish his sentence. Now the killer thought they were together.

"So, it's the killer who has a crush on me," Kristin's tone was light, self-deprecating.

"They might just be trying to get under my skin," he thought aloud.

"So, no one has a crush on me."

"I don't think so," Dan said earnestly, only realizing how it sounded after the words were out of his mouth. "I mean—I'm sure lots of people do, Kristin—just not—maybe not the killer. Probably not exactly a relationship you would want to pursue anyway," he tried to joke, simultaneously grabbing his keys. "I'm coming over," he said, not considering how presumptuous that was or the sheets of hurricane-force rain lashing the road outside. "I need to see this note."

Half an hour later, Dan's headlights swung over Kristin's front yard, highlighting a million droplets of rain in their beams. He pounded up the front steps and the door opened for him. He almost collapsed into the warmth and dryness of her foyer like a man being chased. Kristin stripped his drenched windbreaker from his shoulders, and he wiped at the water coursing down his face.

"Hey," he said breathlessly. "Lovely weather we're having."

After a warm, dry towel-off and a cup of jasmine and honey tea, they stood at Kristin's kitchen counter, comparing her note to the one he'd received and, mentally, to the note he'd found in Mugneret's kitchen. The stationery and penmanship were identical. Had every victim received notes? Which led him down another path entirely: were he and Kristin on the killer's list now? Were they victims-to-be?

Dan stole a glance at Kristin. Her complexion was an unusual alabaster shade, and her eyes bore an almost pitted appearance, nothing at all like the buoyant, rosy face she'd always shown him before. Her hair was swept onto one shoulder, and she stroked it for comfort, staring down at the letter with him.

She was frightened.

Dan swallowed. "I'm going to have to take this to evidence. And we may need to interview you officially. It's even possible Chief may want to stake out your street, or have you watched and tailed, just for the time being."

She stared up at him bleakly. "Okay." There were a few beats of silence in which she seemed to be waiting for him to offer more consolation than he had. But Dan didn't know what else he could tell her. Wasn't the prospect of a bodyguard or two enough to calm her?

"I don't want to sleep here tonight," she said in a rush, her eyes snapping away from him as if she couldn't say it and look at him at the same time. "I don't want to be alone at all. The only protection I have on my front door are a lock with a chain and a keyhole!"

Her lips folded in and clenched, relaxing and parting slightly as a few tears escaped. Then the dam broke. In a moment, she went from massaging her forehead to weeping into her open palms, shoulders shaking. Although she'd seemed remarkably calm up to his moment, Dan realized this wasn't a spontaneous outburst; she had been holding this back for over an hour, since she realized on the phone the "gift" came from a sadistic killer.

Dan stepped forward and wrapped his arms around her, rubbing her quivering shoulders and back. She stayed there for a few seconds as he held her tightly and murmured soothing words and shushing sounds, telling her it was all right (even though they both knew it was not), until she allowed her muscles to relax and her face to fall completely into his shoulder.

They stood like that, semi-rocking back and forth for a minute or two before Kristin peeled away, sniffled deeply, and gazed up at him. "Thanks," she said. Her nose sounded stuffy now. "I needed a good cry. I just—I'm just stressed out."

"You don't need to make excuses for your emotions." He knew all about trying to justify feelings, to shunt personhood to the side in favor of psychobabble and rationalization. He couldn't let Kristin do that to herself. "You're scared. Of course, you're scared." He rubbed her arm and looked down at her, a great sympathy welling in his chest. She looked so miserable with her splotchy cheeks, her eyes still shiny with the runoff of tears. "Why don't we be scared together?" he suggested in what he hoped was a kind voice.

Her bloodshot eyes flicked up to him like she didn't want to believe he really meant it. Like it was too good to be true. "You mean, like a slumber party for people being stalked by serial killers?"

"That's exactly what I mean, although I prefer my wording."

"Me too. That ... that would be really nice, Dan. I don't want to be here alone. At least, if I'm with you, I'll be safe." She stared at him and offered a weak smile.

A sudden impulse to embrace her seized Dan, and he pulled her close once more. His heart throbbed with affection he didn't expect to find in himself. He didn't question it, or feel awkward about it, or even consider it; he just let it be. She was his friend. She was endangered. It was his fault. She hadn't asked for this, and now here she was. It was the only thing to do.

"I really do care about you, Kris," he assured her, pressing a gentle kiss to her forehead. His hand cupped her jawline without a trace of self-awareness, thumb stroking her cheek. "I won't let anything happen to you." He stepped back and his hand fell away.

She blinked up at him with an expression of gratitude and sniffled.

"Come on," he coaxed. "Let's pack you a bag. Hey, do you feel like playing detective with me tonight?"

Every light in Dan's home blazed, even as the clock struck midnight. Wind roared and rain whipped against the walls. Tea brewed. Dan and Kristin pressed against each other's shoulders as they hunched over his library desk, now papered with a clutter of crime scene pictures, essays on the practical usage and history of wine, and tentative lineage trajectories for each of the victims: Amanda Turner, Branden Bullard, Raymond Vasquez, and Sean Mugneret. Each avenue was densely packed with descendants, making it difficult to hold a scent. It had been Kristin's idea to open a bottle of wine, to fuel their creativity. Dan looked at the window in his study. It was shuttered, so whoever lurked outside could not see in, but it also meant they remained unseen. He shook his head and reminded her that creativity wasn't the only thing they needed tonight. They needed focus. They needed fear.

"He's out there, Kris."

"He or she—or they."

Dan considered and nodded. "But probably he. I try to think without gender bias, but there's an eighty-five to ninety percent probability here."

Kristin nodded and pursed her lips. "That explains his little crush on me too."

Dan's brow furrowed and he leaned away from the maps of California and France he'd been analyzing, marking each city in which a body had been located or region where a vineyard was owned.

"First of all," he began, "the killer still could be female—not that she couldn't have a crush on you, of course. Who wouldn't?" He said it with scarcely a thought, and though Kristin blinked, he continued unabashedly. "We haven't seen any positive identifiers of gender; it's possible this killer identifies as neither. We don't know."

"But there is an eighty-five to ninety percent likelihood that this killer has a crush on me," Kristin chuckled.

"The killer does not have a crush on you," Dan said a little too emphatically.

"Why don't you want this killer to have a crush on me so badly?"

"It's not that I don't want the—" Dan looked at her, saw she was grinning, and relaxed. "You're kidding. But it's not funny."

Kristin's smile faltered and fell away. He'd never seen that happen before—all he knew was that he'd taken her smile away.

"I guess you're right," she replied. "Sorry. It's a coping mechanism. I can be serious."

Dan nodded, feeling silly for reprimanding her. "Okay. So we have a probable male, watching the police, contacting at least one detective and his significant other"—he felt Kristin's eyes on him and quickly revised—"assumed significant other. He's selecting victims by a process that seems to be based in heritage and possibly material gain."

Kristin's forehead furrowed. "Okay, we're talking about the killer right now. What do the victims have to do with him psychologically? How do the victims help us identify the killer?"

"His or her motive—"

"But probably his."

"—probably his motive will tell us what type of killer he is," Dan said. "Which makes his or her profile still so fuzzy to us that we can almost say with certainty that he or she is not the conventional serial killer."

"Why is that?"

"Okay. We have killers who feel like they're on a mission. These are religious killings, killings based on discrimination, revenge, perceived injustice, et cetera. It's possible that applies here. There are visionaries, who might believe they've been contacted by God. They suffer from disorders that cause occasional breaks in sanity, like schizophrenia. It's unlikely that applies here, but not impossible. Our killings have been ongoing for a month now. Power and control killers enjoy exerting dominance over another person. That probably doesn't apply. These murders were too clean, their bodies were not abused. Most of them appeared to have died by suicide."

"That isn't a sign of extreme control? Killing people and making it look like it was their will to die?"

Dan nodded. He could see her point. "There are also thrill seekers who kill for the rush, but they choose their victims at random. There are too many connections between these victims for that. And this guy has been in contact with the police, which suggests narcissism and an arrogant amusement at his own genius and our faltering process of investigating the killings. If I had to choose, I'd say our guy, or gal, is none of them, or more than one of them, making him or her more difficult to identify."

"Then let's not look at the victims." Kristin placed her hand over one of the lineage trajectories they had been scribbling down. "Let's look at the crimes. For example, the killer has made contact with you and with me. Maybe he's amused with himself, and his ability to provoke your reactions to what he does. Maybe he's seeing if can predict your reactions. Contacting me probably was a way to yank your chain. So, there is sadism there. And brilliance."

"Above average intelligence is obvious," Dan agreed, "in spite of which he's likely had difficulty functioning in a standard nine-to-five job."

"So, we should be looking for people working brief stints at menial jobs? Maybe a string of different jobs?"

"The killer could also be a creative. An artist, perhaps."

"Sure." Kristin grabbed another sheet of paper and began to scrawl bullet points. "Sadistic. Intelligent."

"No guilt. Aggression. An inability to take responsibility."

"A narcissist," she said, still writing. "I've dated a few of those."

Dan thought about sweet Kristin, trapped in a relationship with a man like that. Of course, they would gravitate toward someone as empathetic and receptive as her; a narcissist could feed on her energy for months. "A voyeur," he added.

Kristin wrote it down.

"We can't overlook his knowledge of—and respect for—wines," Dan continued. "We know he's cultured. He's probably well-traveled. He might be affluent, whether by family money or his own. Sophisticated. Or at the very least, a skilled actor, capable of becoming close to his victims prior to their murders."

"Narcissists and sociopaths often have great acting skills," Kristin said, her eyes scrolling up and down the profile they'd drawn. "I don't want to narrow down your suspect list too much, but this guy sounds exactly like several of my ex-boyfriends."

9

TOO LATE TO SEE LEROY

Alone in his home the next morning after Kristin had left, with the windows shuttered and the alarm system on high, Dan dove deep into his work. By mid-afternoon, he'd leafed through the naturalization records of Amanda's grandmother, who had come to America through New York's Ellis Island as nine-year-old Claire Leroy (1940) before marrying Donovan White of Boston (1951), and giving birth to Amanda's mother, Lydia White (1953), who moved to Los Angeles (around 1974), married Gerald Turner (1985), and gave birth to Amanda Claire Turner (1988). Much further back in time, in the Champagne-Ardenne region of France, Amanda's great-great-grandfather accepted the deed to a vineyard in Burgundy. Dan punctured the exact plot with a pin and wrapped it in red thread, stringing it to New York, where one of Jean-Baptiste Leroy's three adult sons had disembarked with his nine-year-old daughter three quarters of a century earlier.

So, Amanda Turner was Jean-Baptiste Leroy's great-great-granddaughter and heiress to the Leroy plot in Richebourg in Burgundy.

This was insane. It couldn't be right. Dan rechecked the record, then paced back and forth in his study, filled with a kinetic energy, wanting to call

Kristin and at the same time wanting to lock the door and rip all these books apart. He'd been everywhere and nowhere at the same time. The words were starting to run together in his head. Pages upon pages, census records, ship manifests, birth and death records, marriage certificates—he had pulled it all. His hands shook as he marked the Mongeard-Mugneret vineyard with another pin, wrapping it in red thread. Because Sean still bore the surname Mugneret, it wasn't difficult to trace him back to his inheritance, a property in Richebourg, not far from Amanda's Leroy plot. What were the odds that two of his victims could be traced to landowners within a few kilometers of one another?

Dan decided to have a drink. He needed to calm his nerves. There were too many hints and clues percolating in his mind at once. Why had the killer sent Kristin a Riesling, specifically? It was a clue, but to what?

And why were all these victims of French heritage? Did they all own vineyards? Was Vasquez somehow French too? Were these murders financially motivated after all? Then why the notes? They seemed so personal. How had the killer done it? And if they were suicides, which Dan hadn't completely ruled out, how had someone gotten these people to kill themselves in such elaborate, painstakingly connected manners?

Dan tried to shake the thoughts out of his brain and ambled to his basement, on a quest for a suitable wine for his mood. He hadn't thought about the killer watching him at all until he reached the dark door of his cellar. He hesitated, then pushed it open. It was quiet. Of course, that was a good thing, wasn't it?

He walked into the dim, dank atmosphere without further hesitation. No one was here. No one. He'd set all the alarms. "Let's drink to you, Mugneret," Dan said aloud, trying to fill the space with sound. He selected a 2013 Château de la Tour from Clos de Vougeot, then scrambled up the stairs. He grabbed a glass from the kitchen and uncorked the bottle back in the study, pouring the rich red Burgundy into his glass with trembling hands.

He had picked this wine because he remembered going to Clos de Vougeot with Annie. It was in Burgundy, one of the Richebourg vineyards. Like Amanda's great-great-grandfather's plot. Like the Mongeard-Mugneret property. Drinking this wine made him feel closer to the victims—and the killer.

Dan inhaled deeply and conjured a memory from within the glass, calming his frazzled nerves. The last time he had savored these notes, he'd been with Annie in Côte de Nuits. They had struck regal poses together and taken pictures with the charming château of Côte de Nuits over their shoulders. It was surreal to think there had once been a time when his body ached with laughter, pulsed with happiness, lay in repose with deep satisfaction. At the time, those days had seemed as if they would last forever. They'd only just been married. They'd never had any illusions of immortality, but what they knew seemed to sharpen their time together, making everything sweeter.

They had been like wine, in their own way. And now that they had become what they were—corked, sedentary, and purposely avoided—it made perfect sense that he would sometimes need to uncork a bottle, fill a glass, stir the surface and inhale deeply, letting it all take him away. It was only fair. It was all he had left.

Maybe that's how the killer feels. The disturbing little thought flitted through Dan's mind, and he shuddered. But as he moved slowly through the study, the full glass of la Tour gently lapping back and forth, he realized it might not be the worst thing in the world to feel mentally close to the killer. It could be a distinct advantage if he found the strength to embrace it. In most rooms, he was an outsider, a position that could finally be useful to him. He could slip into the killer's mind from here.

They both had far above average IQs. Both had an emotional relationship with the mysterious spirit of wine. How would the killer feel if he were in this study right now, drinking this glass?

If the death scenes of his victims were any indication, he did not process wine the way most people did. He didn't just think of the taste and the price. He didn't even just think about the notes and the process, like some beginners might. He thought of wine's history. He thought of its philosophy. Its elemental underpinnings. Its soul.

Dan savored the Clos de Vougeot and settled down at his desk.

This glass of 2013 Château de la Tour would bring to mind not only the sweet reds and dark fruits but also the strips of vines, the history of the region. Each bottle—and each death—was its own offering to Dionysus, the Greek god of wine, himself. Dan could relate to that spiritual sense of kinship between soil, man, and deity. He could only stand between so many rows of ripe, sun-kissed vines in the buzzing summer twilight before the feeling of kinship leeched into him too. Back when he'd had someone to share it with, wine had been an experience at every level. Every evening in France, flushed and out of breath, he and Annie dove head-first into what each different vineyard had to offer, feeling ancient and immortal with each spirit they imbibed. It was a ritual, a pastime they held in common with the first men and women of civilization.

But that had been so long ago. And they hadn't had the time to hit every plot in Burgundy before moving on; they'd had to cut a hard south to get into Italy on schedule. They'd rushed through the Grivot and Hudelot-Noëllat properties, down into Thibault Liger-Belair and the Domaine de la Romanée-Conti, but they had missed … they'd missed …

Annie's face swam in front of him, an interplay that was almost more shadow than light. "We can't go back and save them anymore," she was saying, her voice like an echo from far away. "There's nothing we can do about that."

She cupped Dan's cheeks, her skin a cool kiss on his, like a nighttime breeze. "We can't save Leroy. It's too late. We can't save Mongeard-Mugneret. But we can still save Romanée-Conti, if we hurry. Let's hurry!" She disappeared through a trim, delicate white pagoda.

The space around him gained dimension. He was no longer in his study. He was in the vineyard, Hudelot-Noëllat, but the trees curved and wavered, rippling with ethereal light. It wasn't normal. It wasn't—

"What did you say?" Dan shouted after her. He felt as if he were getting smaller, fading away. Everything fell into shadows on the sides. It was as if he were in the center of a stage, reciting his monologue, but just realizing that no one was in the audience. The surrounding vineyard grew dark beyond the immediate circumference of his light. "Annie! What did you say?"

"We can't see the Leroy vineyard anymore," she called over her shoulder. "Come on! If we hurry, we can still get to the next winery in time."

He tried to track her with his eyes, but her silhouette was suddenly swimming in an exquisite burst of colorful light. There was no more vineyard at Annie's feet. She was treading confidently into the center of a swirling, prismatic vortex.

Dan wanted to follow her. He wanted to go wherever she was going, even if it wasn't Romanée-Conti, even if it was the gates of hell—

"Annie, wait!" he shouted, but the air itself muffled his voice. Everything was dark and heavy, crowding around him, suffocating him. "Annie!"

The light faded like the last rays of sunset sealing up the horizon, and Annie was gone. Only the dark, sprawling plains of the Richebourg vineyards remained, and Dan stared across the terrain in wonderment, at a loss over what to do next.

Somewhere in the distant sky, a strange chime was sounding at irregular intervals. Dan tried to swat the annoying sound away from his ears as the hills crowded increasingly closer and pressed out all the light, all the air. His arms struggled against the weight of this collapsing world. His eyes bulged open. He had a mouthful of leather, and a nonsensical ding kept ringing through the air. His face was pressed into the neck rest on his swivel chair. He was crushed into an odd position, and he busted out of it, groaning and rubbing his hip. It was the doorbell. Someone was ringing his damn doorbell. What time was it?

Hell, what day was it?

"Hold on," Dan grumbled, shoving himself to his feet. His head dove and sloshed with every movement. He hadn't meant to finish that entire bottle by himself, but there it was, on the desk, empty. He rested the open palm of his hand on his desk. With his other hand he ran fingers through his hair and groaned. He pulled the hand down over his face, letting itself drag his mouth open and his chin down. Damn, he was drunk. He was drunk, but he'd also just had a kind of amazing moment.

The doorbell finally stopped ringing.

Whoever had been standing on his stoop must have gone away.

His honeymoon with Annie had been so long ago now, and he'd spent the past two years running from everything that smelled of Annie, sounded like Annie, felt like Annie. He'd blocked out entire days of his life—the best days of his life. Those windows stayed dark now. But he'd seen them clearly in his dream, the vineyards they had been forced to skip, the names he'd discarded to the sands of time. But now he saw.

The lineage trajectory maps soared into southeastern France, flagging the domaines of Burgundy. The victims—Amanda Turner (of Leroy heritage), Branden Bullard (of the Camuzet line), Raymond Vasquez (of the Thibault Liger-Belair tree), and Sean Mugneret (of the Mongeard-Mugnerets)—were all heirs to vineyards in Richebourg. That was how the killer was selecting his victims.

Distantly, quietly, his front door opened, but he didn't hear it.

"It's a—it's a—" His eyes ticked over the desk as he tried to conjure the right term for it. The inheritance laws of the Richebourg plots didn't make this a grab for land. It couldn't possibly be; he or she would need to kill a hundred people to erase it all.

Footsteps approached from down the hall, but they didn't register.

"It's a vendetta," he realized, standing as if he were going to launch himself off his desk and go tell the world. He took a few long strides before recalling that he was drunk. The room around him curved and swooned. "It's a vendetta."

"Hey, Dan." A familiar voice called from the hallway, and Dan froze, as if he'd been caught in the act of some crime. It was Rachel Porter. Sweet, innocent Rachel. And here he was, drunk and alone for the first time since he was a teenager. Here he was, stinking like a man obsessed. His clothes were loose and wrinkled; he had just woken from a dream in his swivel chair, and he looked like it. The desk behind him overflowed with disorganized fact sheets, and the wall was dominated by two maps, one of Europe and another of the US, with multicolored strings tied back and forth between the pins on each of them to show the movement of each victim's ancestors over the years.

He would have preferred it be anyone else—even Kristin. At least Kristin knew and accepted that he was a mess. But all he ever did was reassure Rachel that she was wrong, that he didn't need grief counseling or a sabbatical from the force.

She gazed at him as if he were a sick dog that she needed to take to the vet … and have put down.

"Rachel." Dan tried to strike a pose that looked natural and sober. She stared at him bleakly. "What are you doing here?"

"We came to surprise you. Boris is getting the dinner out of our car. It's—we made chili and nachos. I got worried when you didn't answer the door. It's seven o'clock, Dan." She cleared her throat. "Friday."

"I know what day it is."

"We made the guacamole from scratch," she said delicately. "Did you already eat?"

He could practically hear her begging him to say yes, so she could at least justify his drunkenness as a misstep from dinner, but Dan shook his head. He couldn't lie to her—not anymore. Not tonight. He had reached his maximum capacity for secrets and lies. "No, I did not," he said. "I was going to—Chinatown has the most perfect goose, which is ironic, you know, because it's Chinatown, dealing in the delicacies of Burgundy, and I've already got the Camembert—but then I forgot. I got caught up." He gestured to the madman's den directly behind him. "In work stuff," he explained limply.

Rachel nodded, peering at him seriously. "You don't look good. I felt like we saw each other not so long ago, but maybe it has been a while."

It had been another two weeks. Technically, that wasn't too long at all, but he did feel older in spite of it. He couldn't even paraphrase everything that had happened since he'd seen her squeezing avocados in the produce aisle.

"It's a long story," he said.

Rachel nodded to the web of red string behind him. "I can see that."

"Rach?" Boris's voice floated down the hallway toward them. He was hunting with his eyes, traveling down the corridor in their direction, the dim muffle of their voices drawing him onward. "Daa-aan?"

"We're in here," Rachel called.

Boris broke through the study door behind her, holding a tray of elaborate dip. "I left the chips in the kitchen." Boris nudged Dan and grinned. "So, what are we all doing in here?" He looked toward the cluttered wall and desk, and his brow creased as he glanced back at Dan. "Is this all about your case?"

"My cases," Dan said. "Now there are four of them."

"Let's go to the dining room," Rachel said, her tone soft and her eyes huge, tracking Dan as though she thought he might crumble or explode. "Let's talk. We haven't seen you in forever."

Dan allowed them to lead him into the dining room, where a high stack of pita chips waited for them on a tray shaped like a conch shell. Boris uncloaked their seven-layer dip, complete with beans, guacamole, corn, salsa, sour cream, and a crust of peppers and cheese.

"This looks delicious," Dan said, trying not to slur.

Rachel pursed her lips. "Your boss is overloading you with work," she practically whispered. "It's not fair to you. You need a dedicated team under you, doing this work with you and for you, so you don't end up looking like —like—"

A half-smile curled at the corner of Dan's mouth. "Like what?"

"Like a crazy person." She blurted the words with force, going against her nature of sugarcoating the truth.

"I don't want help," Dan replied caustically, even knowing how crazy that bitter response made him sound. "I want to do it alone. Other people just get in the way."

"That makes you sound crazy too," Rachel said.

Dan felt anger flushing up in his chest, and even though he knew he was still drunk, he couldn't stop himself. "Say what you want. You don't know what it's like. These people died." The veins on his neck bulged against his skin. "This person—they've killed four people." He tapped the table four times. Then he leaned across the table, lowering his voice. "They've made direct contact with me, so I know I'm on the right track, and I can't risk—I cannot risk missing another beat."

"You can't afford to miss too much more sleep either," Boris said. "It's taking a serious toll on you, Dan. Your body will force you to sleep, you know. In battles of self-imposed sleep deprivation, the human body always wins."

"The killer contacted you directly?" Rachel blurted. "When? How?" Her eyes darted to the window. The luscious-looking seven-layer dip remained untouched. "Does he know where you live?"

"He knows where I live, and he's been watching me. He contacted Kris too. Threatened her."

Boris and Rachel exchanged a look, and then faced him again. "Kris?" she said. "Who's Kris?"

Dan pinched himself mentally. "Kristin Meyers," he answered as lightly as possible. "An old friend of mine from about fifteen years ago when I thought I might be a master sommelier someday." There was a moment of silence. Boris and Rachel smiled at him. "It's strictly professional," he added, though he wasn't sure exactly why.

Rachel tentatively plucked a pita chip from the tray and dipped it. "So, is she pretty?" she asked, momentarily distracted from her earlier worry, her tone twice as light as Dan's had been.

"No," Dan answered, deadpan. He did not need to be discussing this with anyone, especially not Rachel, who was so eager to help him "move on" from Annie. She didn't get it; her good intentions had blinded her. There was no getting over a loss like Annie. There was only survival. Just living to the next day was all he could do. He wasn't going to work reasonable hours. He wasn't going to start sleeping more and jogging again. And he sure as hell wasn't going to be dating anybody anytime soon.

Dan resisted the urge to call Kristin for the entire weekend. He buried himself in tracing lineages until he came away from his hours of research with one family member he could pinpoint at the purchase of a domaine in Richebourg. Until then he had found himself looking at an almost entirely staked territory. Frantin, a sliver of northern vineyard in the Richebourg plot; Grivot; and the famed, massive Romanée-Conti were all that remained untouched by pins and red string.

Dan tipped a glass of red to his lips without bothering to swish or sniff at it. He drank it the way a problem drinker drinks: quickly and without frills. Accordingly, it sloshed too hard against his lips and broke over the top of the glass, dripping down his fingers. He brought his glass down with a muttered curse and went to mop at his hand, glaring, unshaken from the dilemma of those maps up there. All that red string. He felt tangled in it now.

He had connected America to France—but he needed to connect France back to America. He had to bring the maps down and start tracing lineage forward, not backward. He needed to find descendants now, not ancestors. He knew he needed American citizens now. This killer seemed to be operating solely in California.

But when had the killer stopped selecting from a group of friends? After all, he had chosen Mugneret and broken the pattern, hadn't he? What if the next murder took place in France? Dan needed to be sure …

Mapping out the dozens of children seeded from the original spore of Frantin, Grivot, and Romanée-Conti took the rest of the weekend and produced lackluster results. He couldn't trace anyone to California. He could barely find a link to the country. The Frantin line, to this day, resided in the village of Richebourg. He couldn't find anyone from Romanée-Conti after 2008. Although he did find a family connected to Grivot all along the East Coast of the US, they were scattered from New York to Florida; it was impossible to pick where to begin.

Dan closed his eyes and exhaled, trying to center himself.

Annie materialized behind his eyelids, and his heart gave up a sharp throb, wishing hard she was with him now. She was such a thinker, a planner. Her attitude was positive and persistent. God, he'd loved her. She'd made life so much brighter just by her presence. And now, here he was, drinking and staring at maps until they blurred, trying to put himself into the shoes of a killer. It was the best idea he had, and it was a good one, but it was driving him insane.

She'd been a people person. She could have cracked anyone. And she had common sense, with a memory like a bear trap.

"Give me a sign, help me," Dan begged her, as if she hovered in the ether. Sometimes it felt as if she did. He exhaled and felt a little silly and a little sad, but at the same time, this tiny part of his heart believed. "Give me a sign."

He imagined the heirs of the Grivot, Frantin, and Romanée-Conti domaines, and which one of them might taste like Riesling.

Unless, that is, he was fully wrong about the killer's method for selecting his victims, and even wrong about his motive. What if there was no vendetta? What if there was nothing but the thrill of it all, the exertion of power, the mockery of the foolish police? What if the next most likely target was Kristin?

Dan scooped up his glass of red off the map of America.

The stained stem from his spill had left a bright red ring around New York, where Simone Oberman, great-great-granddaughter of the original landowner, was currently studying at Juilliard.

Dan stared at the blurry crimson circle around Simone's name.

"Did I do that," he wondered into the air, "or did you?"

He couldn't jump to any conclusions just yet. He would need to start making calls first. But he would start with Simone Oberman, the Grivot descendant whose name stood centered in a blurry red circle, like a bull's eye.

10

NAGGING NOTE REVISITED

S imone Oberman's number was in the middle of its second ring when the phone picked up. "Jacques?" a panicked female voice strangled across the line.

Dan's eyes widened in thought. Jacques? "Um, no," Dan replied. "May I speak to Ms. Simone Oberman, please?"

"Speaking," Simone replied, her tone chilling and tightening now that she had ascertained this was not Jacques.

"My name is Detective Winters. I'm with the San Francisco PD. I was wondering if I could ask you a few questions."

"Now?" She sounded distraught. "I don't know. How do I know you are who you say you are? What is this in reference to?"

Dan gave her his badge number and forwarded her his agency webpage, where she could learn about where he had gone to college and how long he'd been a detective. She could even see a picture of his wooden smile, as he stood in front of a blue backdrop. Simone said that she was going to check immediately, and Dan heard what sounded like tapping on a keyboard in the background.

"So," Dan said casually, "is Jacques your boyfriend?"

"I still don't know why you're calling, detective." There was a subtle sniff in her voice. Dan wondered if she was looking at his pictures and all his credentials right now, weighing how much she wanted to say, or if she just wanted to make this difficult for him.

"Ah, yes, Ms. Oberman," Dan obliged her. "You're right." Difficult witnesses were much easier to handle when he treated them like small children. You had to keep a cool head and let them always feel they were the ones making the choices. "There has been a string of four related murders in the Bay area, and we're connecting the victims through their heritage, some of which you share."

A moment of silence was followed by a dry, "Fascinating," and another moment. "What a juicy theory." Her voice was deadpan, and Dan suspected she was screwing with him. "What does this have to do with me again?"

"We wanted to reach out to you and see if anyone new, unusual, or suspicious might have been in contact with you recently."

"Because of my heritage," she snipped with a mocking cheerfulness. "Someone is slaughtering French Americans. Four so far. What are the odds?" She sounded amused now. "You know, I've heard that white people do often spend time together, socializing."

"It is a little more complicated than that," Dan replied good-naturedly. "These victims have actually been pinpointed to a specific plot of land in France."

"Huh. That must be my mom's side of the family. She died when I was a baby. My dad is mostly German. Some Swiss, I think—"

"I couldn't help but notice that you were expecting a call from a man named Jacques," Dan went on. "That's a pretty traditional French name."

Simone scoffed, a tad awkwardly, Dan thought. "I, um, I don't know who you're talking about."

"Jacques, the man whose name you said when you first picked up the phone."

"I don't recall saying that."

Dan frowned. He was certain she was lying but trying to sound confident. So, she was a good liar. He found himself wondering what she smelled like, lamenting that this exchange was taking place over their phones. Scent could have revealed the missing key from her tone.

"You've met no one named Jacques?"

"This is badgering the witness."

"There's no judge here."

Click.

Dan lowered his phone, his thoughts distant and musing. She had said Jacques. He was sure of it.

He tried to call her back. Seven times. Each was forwarded to an answering machine.

Dan didn't bring Simone Oberman to Chief's attention because he knew what Chief would say. Simone Oberman was New York City's problem, and they would have to communicate interdepartmentally to move forward within protocol. But Dan didn't trust other people like that; they'd treat this fragile lead clumsily and lose it—or break it. Simone was communicating with the killer; her evasiveness made him confident of that. Time was critical.

So, he did the only thing he could do, according to his moral and professional standards. He took his vacation time for the week and bought a plane ticket to New York City. Anyone who knew him at all would know he was hiding something.

"What are you talking about—your vacation time?" Chief spat at him from across his desk. "Right now? In the middle of the hottest case you've ever had?"

Dan's nostril twitched. Chief smelled more acrid than normal today. He was sweat, and cheap aftershave, and French fry grease, but under all that—in his fingernails—clung a medicinal odor, alcohol, with a dirty whiff of nicotine. Dan guessed he was smoking again, and he was ashamed about it. He had sneaked a cigarette outdoors, then bathed his hands in sanitizer to disguise one odor quickly with another—but he couldn't hide it from Dan.

"Do you smell smoke?" Dan asked, trying to distract Chief while gaining some advantage in this conversation. His tone was warm, curious, and innocent, but he knew his eyes gave away his triumphant knowledge.

"I don't smell anything like that."

"Huh. That's the craziest thing. I smell cigarette smoke on fingertips. And —rubbing alcohol? Ugh."

"You can smell that?"

"Sure can. Wasn't your wife the one who made you quit smoking, Chief? Boy, I'd hate to be in the room if she found out somehow."

Chief's eyebrows lowered as he said he'd approve the time off and he needed to go to the lockers for a second.

Dan touched down at JFK on Tuesday night, rented a car and got a hotel room. He told himself that he needed sleep to be alert, but he was wired all night. Eventually, he stopped fighting the adrenaline and insomnia, and at dawn, he drove his rental to the suburbs, where Simone Oberman lived in her single-bedroom house.

Her home was a complicated structure of tinted glass and brick, almost extravagant for the lonely and driven life she seemed to be leading; she was a violinist, pursuing her Master's, and the only evidence of a love or social life had been that one strangled word over the phone—"Jacques?" She could have lived just as efficiently in any cookie-cutter apartment, but here she was, in her own home, with a manicured yard and big windows. She must have come from money. This was a quiet family neighborhood; it was almost dawn, and everything was utterly silent, except for the soft rumbling and turning of car engines as diligent worker bees flipped on their headlights and trundled down their driveways in reverse.

Meanwhile, Dan sat across from Simone Oberman's home at eight o'clock in the morning and watched her profile flash from one window to the next. He had never seen her before this moment. She swept past one window in a cream-colored bra, her face hidden behind a curtain of richly curled hair the color of cocoa, like Amanda's. Her skin tone was a warm olive. She flipped the hair off her shoulder, and he caught a brief flash of her face: delicate cheekbones, slim nose, shrewd eyes, heavy eyebrows, nonexistent lips. Her face was small and oddly pointed. She wasn't wearing any makeup. She looked serious, like an actress in a silent film.

The next time Simone darted along a series of windows, her hair had been tied to the side, and she wore a slinky black tank top with a thin, rose-patterned robe. A full red lip, a little blush, and smoky eyes worked hard to soften her features. She was beautiful. He wondered at the panicked tone in her voice when she had called out for Jacques, a man she immediately claimed to not know. Who was she protecting? Why?

How could he get her to let him in?

The garage door shuddered open, and a black Jeep came rolling out. Dan followed at a pace of several vehicles, all the way to the crowded campus of Juilliard.

He drove after her to a building called Sky Lab. There, he waited until Simone was at a sufficient distance before he climbed from the vehicle and kept behind her. She had seen him before, a few days earlier, but only in a photo. Still, he lagged. He could now see in detail what she was wearing today, having ditched the robe for something more professional: a green silk blouse tucked into high-waisted, loose black pants. She looked sophisticated, as a classical musician should, as Dan watched her go into the Sky Lab.

He waited a minute, pretending to check his phone, and then headed inside. A young male receptionist glanced at him and offered a small smile. The large room wreaked of fresh flowers, fresh paper, and the obnoxious aftertaste of cinnamon-apple deodorizer plugged into an outlet somewhere nearby. But this apple-cheeked college kid, with his neatly kept beard and immaculate blond shag, smelled primarily of inexpensive Axe cologne as well as … nutmeg and chocolate.

"Hello, how can I help you?" the boy asked. His little plaque said his name was Benjamin.

"I was passing by, and I'm actually just—curious," Dan explained. "What is this place?"

"Sky Lab is one of Juilliard's most exciting new projects," Benjamin smiled. It was too early for all this chit-chat. Dan stepped closer to the desk and saw the source of the nutmeg and chocolate aroma: a cold mocha, probably from hours ago, sat with its lid still on, behind the desk. No wonder Benjamin was so chipper. "We're using the latest technology to bring the most vivid and engaging tutorials to students around the globe. We've got five classes in progress right now."

"Taught by students, as well as teachers?"

"More students than teachers, actually," Benjamin said. "We have a lot of introductory courses that we let our graduate students teach for us. It's difficult to teach intense lessons long-distance, but the basics are simple enough. The young woman who entered the building ahead of you is one of our teachers. I don't know if you saw her. She's a violinist."

Dan always found it disturbing how quickly people would give up information about strangers to other strangers. This morning, Benjamin's oversight would work to Dan's benefit.

"Would you like to ask Ms. Oberman some questions when this class concludes? Do you have a teaching license? We're not accepting applicants at the moment, but Sky Lab is going to receive a grant to expand substantially within the next five years. We hope to draw from a wide pool of supporters."

"Absolutely," Dan lied with enthusiasm. He asked if it was okay for him to just look around by himself, and Benjamin allowed that it was. Dan walked and glanced through the windows until he found the willowy Ms. Oberman sitting behind a simple desk in front of several cameras. He watched her without thinking that she might look up and see him at any moment. Her eyes were locked on the camera. She frequently produced a violin from behind her desk and played it to illustrate a point.

He smelled the approaching delivery woman before he saw her.

The middle-aged woman was rank with citrus rinds, a juicy, succulent, fresh aroma that wreathed her from head to toe like some springtime goddess. She was just a delivery person in simple brown slacks and a button-down shirt, but she was holding a metallic basket filled with lemons and limes, peaches, and apples.

Dan's eyes glazed over as the woman stepped past him. She reached for the doorknob and Dan instinctively gripped her forearm, eyes bulging. He swallowed thickly. "What is this?"

"Uh … a fruit basket," the woman replied, staring back at him. "I work for Gloria's Custom Gifts."

"Who is it from?

The delivery woman slanted her mouth to the side. "I don't know."

"You don't know?"

The woman glared at Dan and half shrugged. "Haven't you ever heard of a secret admirer?" Looked like she hadn't had any kind of nutmeg mocha or secret admirer today herself. "I don't think they've taken that away from us yet."

Dan couldn't smell this woman too clearly with all the citrus interference, but he could still use his eyes, and her demeanor screamed hostility. She was not going to let him see the card attached to a holder which neatly speared one lemon. But she might let him just look at the basket for a second.

"May I see that?" Dan asked, trying to sound as naïve and innocuous as he could. "I've never seen such a unique fruit basket and my—my wife loves fruit. I might have to send one to her work." The lie flowed easily out of

Dan, though the mental image of Annie being at work again sent a hard pang reverberating through him.

The woman surveyed Dan in turn, then grimaced and reluctantly handed him the basket. "Most of our baskets are wicker, just so you know," she said offhandedly. "But, uh, this client insisted on metal."

Dan braced the chilly basket—more of a bird cage than a basket, really—and deeply inhaled the aroma within, closing his eyes to truly let the elements mix beneath the surface of his consciousness. He could almost see the vineyard now. The pale grapes, braced by winter. The vibrant summer flavors, tart, nearly abrasive. He could visualize the wine in the glass itself, feel it in his hand, hear it swirl. Come on, come on, come on. Who are you?

Just as the clouds were about to part and show him the wine—something was missing, what was it?—the woman took back her basket. She pushed the classroom door open with her foot, and as she shouldered the massive basket into the fake classroom, Dan saw a flash of the insides of the folded note: *"Bon appétit."*

The woman carefully placed the gift onto a table outside the camera's radius and Simone's eyes fluttered to it without breaking her concentration on the task at hand. Dan watched helplessly, fighting the strong urge to burst in and flee with the damn basket. But he had no sound excuse to do so. He had to just watch—and think as fast as he could.

What was the missing note in that bouquet? What was the wine? What was "Jacques" trying to tell her?

The lesson concluded, Dan guessed, by the way Simone stood and smoothed her blouse, tucking away the violin and striding to the table with the basket. She seemed delighted; it was surreal to think simple fruit might be dangerous, and for one split second, Dan felt silly. Here this woman was, a promising violinist with a tenuous tie to a plot of French land, thanking this delivery woman for her gift basket in such a banal way. This kind of thing happened every day. No one ever died. What if Simone just opened the cage, plucked an apple from inside, took a bite, smiled, tipped the delivery lady, and went back to teaching her next lesson? What if Dan was wrong about every—

Simone extracted the note from its holder and flipped it open.

As soon as she did, he saw how her face changed, and his blood ran cold. He hadn't been wrong. He'd been right. About everything.

Her eyelids drooped. The difference was only a fraction, but there it was. He saw it happen. The smile smoothed off her lips; she picked up the basket from the table and fled toward the back of the classroom. She didn't say anything to the delivery woman. Simone pushed through a back door and disappeared with her spoils.

Dan gaped after her for a second. It was all happening too quickly. He wasn't prepared. He thought he would have more time. He sprang into action, wrenching the handle on the classroom door and bolting onto the set.

"Hey!" some camera guy called. The room was unnaturally clean, so the only scents Dan could register were that of the basket and the people in the room. Camera Guy smelled like menthol and lemon and, underneath it all, phlegm. He was sick. "Dude. Get out of the shot."

Dan glanced in the general direction of the voice, didn't even really register the man's face, and bolted toward the back door. No one was fast enough to follow close behind him, and he chased the fading aroma of the basket all the way through Sky Lab's circuitous halls until he found himself at the parking lot again.

Just in time to see Simone's car peel past him, the basket in her passenger seat.

But the most vital detail in this moment wasn't the bland, mindless smile on Simone's lips, and it wasn't the faded symphony of oranges, limes, apples, and peaches. It was the mixture of all that with the exhaust from Simone's vehicle. The gas.

Riesling.

Of course. Kristin!

The killer hadn't been threatening Kristin. He or she had been leaving a clue—for Dan.

And now, was it too late?

If the only missing element of the bouquet was gas, where might Simone go? Was she about to commit suicide? Could a person change that quickly, end their life on a pivot when only moments before, they'd been teaching a class and accepting gifts on a typical Tuesday?

Dan didn't know. He climbed into his car and careened from the Sky Lab lot into the congested throng of New York City morning traffic.

Almost an hour later, Dan arrived at Simone's suburban rancher again, his lone consolation being that she couldn't possibly have arrived much earlier than he had. Still, he parked on the street and bolted into the house. How long did it really take to kill yourself? It depended on the method. And if she wanted to recreate the signature odor of Riesling, that aftertaste of gasoline—

Dan found her front door unlocked and went immediately to the garage. Exhaust rolled out on top of him, and he coughed, spluttered, and gagged, unable to bear the overwhelming assault on his senses. His eyes filled with tears, and he forced himself into the swath of fog, barely able to discern her vehicle.

"Simone!" Dan yelled, charging through the ether and banging on the driver's door of her car. She had reclined her seat and seemed to be in a deep, peaceful slumber. Dan couldn't tell if she was alive or dead. He tried the door handle: locked.

In the extreme smog, he hacked and groped for some kind of weapon, located a crowbar among some tools, and came back with a powerful blow to the glass. It shattered on impact and Dan reached into the car, unlocked the door, pulled it open, and collected Simone's limp body from inside. Her eyes didn't open, but her throat spasmed softly as she let one small cough loose. She was still alive, but just barely.

Dan's skin burned with the acidity of the gasoline as he made his way to the garage door, sloppily toggling its power switch and opening the wide door. It was so slow. He hacked and wept without control against the burning fumes. The smoke filtered out through the bottom of the door quickly, and sunlight fell on their faces. Dan staggered from the garage and hit his knees, spilling Simone onto the concrete. Fresh air poured into his lungs, but Simone hardly stirred.

He palmed his cell phone from his pocket and dialed 9-1-1. Then he opened the top two buttons on her blouse and pressed his ear to her sternum. Her heartbeat was faint and irregular, but she was still breathing. He could hear her wheeze too; her lungs were weak. They would have to hurry. There was too much smoke in her system. Once he explained the situation and his detective status, the operator transferred him to someone who promised they were sending a specialized ambulance that was outfitted with a hyperbaric chamber. She would be fine, they promised. He could calm down.

But Dan just sat on the pavement, this limp woman lying at his feet, with the urge to sob culminating in his chest until it was impossible to suppress any longer. He bowed his head, and his shoulders shook as silent tears fell from his eyes. But beneath the raging competition of anxiety and horror was another emotion, strong and low and persistent, just like the gas in a finely aged Riesling: relief. Softer still was the notion of victory in every tear that dropped down his cheek. Not just relief. Victory.

He'd done it. He had saved this one. He hadn't let Chief prevent him from coming. He hadn't let Simone's reluctance stop him. He had shouldered through every door alone.

The sound of the sirens brought him out of his own thoughts. He wiped the tears from his cheeks and took a deep breath. An impressive commotion swelled around him as a team of medics rushed forward to collect Simone from the driveway. After reassuring him that she would be fine, they took his information and let him know they would be in contact. Simone was put on a stretcher and rolled away. Dan watched as they loaded her onto the ambulance and took off.

The red and white van became smaller and smaller, became quieter, became a speck down the road, and then disappeared, leaving Dan standing alone in someone else's driveway, someone else's suburb, someone else's garage door still hanging open—but the smoke was almost clear, and unless you had a nose like Dan's, you would be tempted to think that nothing had happened here at all.

※

"I'm still confused," Chief grumbled on the other end of the phone line. Dan had been dreading this call all day, but he couldn't avoid it any longer. Too much was happening, and Chief needed to know. "You took your vacation time and used it to go to New York for your case?"

"Yes," Dan said, hoping to gloss over the question in the same way he'd disregarded Chief's authority. "And my hunch was correct. Simone Oberman had indeed been contacted by our killer. She attempted suicide right in front of me."

"All right, all right," Chief said, though he seemed only to be saying it to shut Dan up. "You need to talk to this girl if she really is relevant. We need words on record, or we can't do shit with this shit."

"I can do that," Dan promised, though he wasn't sure. "I can tell you I think I understand the killer's method now."

"Please don't let it be some fruity nonsense," Chief replied almost inaudibly. "All right, Magic, what have you got for me?"

"Hypnosis."

Chief muttered an oath. "Hypnosis. You've got to be kidding."

"Triggered with the phrase "*bon appétit.*" The only thing I can't figure out is how the killer is setting the trigger phrase in the victim's minds."

There was silence on the line for several moments. "Hypnosis. That's going to be one hell of a murder weapon to prove—you know that, right?"

"We already have one witness," Dan chirped. "She mentioned a man named Jacques to me. But then, when I asked her about it later, she acted like she didn't know anyone named Jacques. I don't know if she just lied, or if she really didn't remember him anymore."

"She was lying," Chief said, deadpan. "They always do. Talk to the girl and get back here. We'll see what we can do with this mess. Are you sure it's hypnosis, Winters?"

Dan nodded to himself. "You didn't see her face when she read the card. Her eyes changed. The expression all drained away. It was like she fell asleep. Instantly."

"Maybe," Chief allowed. "Question the girl. Get back here. We'll talk then. And stop wasting your damn vacation time, boy."

Dan hung up the call and sat alone in his room, thinking.

A few hours after the ambulance had come and gone, Dan received a call from one of the medics informing him that Simone was unconscious but stable, and they were expecting her to wake up any minute.

By now, the killer probably realized Simone Oberman was still alive.

Dan wondered if the killer also knew why. If he or she knew Dan was here. If the killer could see him, with that preternatural eye he seemed to have. The same preternatural eye that had led the killer to his stoop in the first place. At the time, Dan had extracted each bottle, examining it in the light.

The first was an earthy, rich red, labeled Coonawarra.

Next, a Rhône Valley Syrah.

Then, a Friulano.

When the bottles were out, he ducked his head inside, but there was nothing there, save one small note, a folded tab of stiff, creamy parchment, with a small filigree edging the borders. The message inside was handwritten in spiky black penmanship, delicate and wild. It read, *"Bon appétit."*

Dan swallowed and stared numbly out the hotel room window at the sprawling city beyond. A million lights. And so many shadows.

Were they out there somewhere, watching him? Waiting to send him his own fateful basket of fruits and flowers?

11

GHOSTS OF RICHEBOURG

Dan tried not to smell hospitals too deeply. There was nothing to be gained from the slog of antibacterial soap and alcohol and decay and blood, all mixed together. It was enough to make a man sick. Working in a restaurant had pushed his olfactory skills to their limits; working at a hospital would have driven him insane. But he'd had to come because Simone was reportedly awake now. He had to catch her before they let her sign herself out, if they did, because he suspected that, once she was gone, she would be as hard to catch as a fish in the ocean.

When Dan arrived at her room, she was napping, so he pulled a magazine from the waiting room across the hall and sat in wait. Almost an hour later, she awoke, her eyelids heavy, eyes glazed with confusion and half-sleep. Gone was her perfect makeup, hair, and clothing, replaced by limp dark strands and tired, sallow skin, paired with a paper-like gown. And she still smelled faintly of exhaust.

But she was at least open to a conversation with the man who had saved her—until a few moments later when she learned that he was the nosey man on the phone few days ago.

"Hey, Simone," Dan greeted her gently, as if she was a sick child.

Simone glared at him from her hospital bed. She was still on oxygen. "Ms. Oberman, please."

"Right," Dan agreed, sticking out a hand for her to take. She had almost died yesterday. He could understand a little moodiness. "My name's Detective Daniel Winters." She looked at his hand with a sour mouth.

"You're the one who broke into my house—"

"Uh, and extracted you from a garage filled with carbon monoxide."

"—and broke my car's window." Her version of reality was vastly different from his, he could see. "I wonder if my insurance covers vigilantism."

Dan stared at her wryly. "I'm here to ask you some questions regarding that basket of fruit you received."

Simone looked at him flatly. "What basket?"

Dan sighed. "Let's not play this game again. We already had a round when you said you didn't know anyone named Jacques. There are no winners in this game."

"Again," Simone seethed, "I do not know who you're talking about. I don't know any Jacques, and I don't recall any … fruit basket."

How could she not remember? She had seemed so genuine.

Dan knew when to give up, so he bade Simone farewell, returned to his hotel room, and then went to the airport, where he pulled out his laptop and trudged through all his data on the ancestor and descendant lines. He couldn't find any Jacques currently alive. But if the only two vineyards still standing with zero attached victims were now the Frantin and the Romanée-Conti—the smallest and the largest of the Richebourg plots—Dan wondered if Jacques, the alleged killer, might have been from one of those two lineages.

He could hardly pause from his research to board the plane home to San Francisco. Even on the plane, he was perusing the notes on his laptop, none of which led to anyone named Jacques. It couldn't have been a coincidence, could it? How could it possibly be insignificant that Simone had mentioned the name—and then seemed to forget it, unable to recall it again? What did that mean? Was Jacques even real?

Dan had to give up the tentative lead to the rules of common sense, and he returned to San Francisco almost empty-handed—except for having saved Simone Oberman's life.

No one had ever visited Dan at work before except Annie, so when he heard Manozza announce, "Dan, you've got company," he almost wanted to rebut that no one knew he even worked here. But then Manozza clapped him on the shoulder and added conspiratorially, "You dog." He gave Dan's shoulder a little squeeze and Dan's eyes followed his wolfish gaze to the curvaceous redhead seated by his desk. Dan swallowed. It was Kristin. Her hair was richly layered today—she must have just been to the salon—and she wore a navy-blue dress snug in the torso with a flared hem in a style from the sixties. The neckline scooped over her breasts in a way that was both classy and provocative. You couldn't see anything, but you were pretty sure you wanted to.

"Hey, Dan," Kristin chirped when her eyes lit on him. She didn't get up, but she did lean in toward him. "I just wanted to come by and let you know you're taking me to a wine tasting tonight at Top Drawer. They're showcasing the stars of Burgundy, and I thought it might help open your mind up. I even took a night off work for this occasion! I don't want you to be late picking me up. Come by at seven!"

She stood and leaned, pressing close for a big hug. "Congratulations," she breathed, her voice brimming with actual joy. "You saved that girl's life, tiger." She pulled away again and punched him lightly on the arm. "See you at seven."

Dan watched her go with a slackness in his jaw that he barely remembered to pull back up.

The sky that night seemed to sprawl in every direction. Dan had a feeling like static electricity running through the fibers of his body: it was mostly dark in the winery, but he could feel the slightest brush of a touch and the sparkle and mild heat of something … happening. He didn't know where it was coming from, and he didn't examine it too closely. It felt good, and he thought if he looked too closely, it might fade away.

Top Drawer was a small, dimly lit winery overlooking one of San Francisco's many coves. As soon as Dan crossed the threshold, he was embraced by the warm interplay of light, shadow, and delicate tinkling of piano keys, and his eyes trailed to Kristin and caught her gaze. She was the first person in the room he really saw; she seemed gilded in light, while everyone else was just there as a backdrop. Her hair was knotted on top of her head in a complicated beehive, and she wore a gold-and-black patterned sheath dress. Her neck, wrists, and ears glimmered with jewels. One of them winked at Dan as she waved him over, grinning.

"Tell me the entire story all over again, from the very beginning," she gushed as soon as he was within earshot. She crossed the winery floor and her hand slid over his arm. She beamed up at him proudly. "I can't believe you saved that woman's life with minutes to spare. Seconds."

"You're being dramatic," Dan said with a self-conscious laugh. "What are you drinking there?"

"Oh, this?" She gestured at her glass. "A nice Chambolle. Stop changing the subject!" She laughed, swatting him with her free hand.

Dan grinned and blushed slightly. Was she always this touchy? That was the damn thing. She was.

She blinked up at him expectantly. "So, tell me, did you discover anything really valuable while you were there?"

"Just what I already told you, about how the girl was triggered by a letter. Well, and—" Dan thought more seriously and decided that the detail about Jacques wouldn't be important until he could find an actual person to associate with the name. "Well, nothing."

"What?" Kristin persisted.

"You're relentless, you know that? Okay, the victim said a man's name to me—Jacques, she called me Jacques accidentally—but then, she denied it, and said she didn't know who Jacques was. I can't find a Jacques anywhere in these families, though. No Jacques associated with Richebourg at all right now."

He shrugged and shook his head. Feeling impulsive and playful now that he was with her, he lightly took her wine glass, swirled it, and brought the delicate red to his nose for a whiff. "Oh, well. Do you know any Jacques, Kristin?" His tone was purposely languishing, as if he might as well just ask everyone in the country if they knew anyone named Jacques.

Kristin's eyes crinkled as she grinned. "As a matter of fact, I do. Just one. There is Jacques Stevens, food critic. You know him too. I had no idea his background in wine was so dark, though."

"Jack Stevens."

"Oh, I know what his name is. I'm just playing around. Can you imagine him, tapping out his 'SF Cornucopia' articles on, like, a throne of skulls?" She giggled, clearly having forgotten that she was comparing him to a real murderer. "He's such a cute little guy. Can I have my glass back?"

"Of course," Dan said, offering her the glass and a smile, even though his mind was thousands of miles away right now, wondering where Jack Stevens was originally from.

The night passed too quickly for Dan's tastes, which was not something he was accustomed to feeling. Kristin was so vibrant that the owner of Top Drawer offered her a job as their sommelier, which she graciously declined. The many wines of Burgundy Dan tasted left him feeling altered, emotionally and mentally, as if he were someone else.

At home, he traveled online to the San Francisco tourism website, which linked to Jack's "SF Cornucopia" articles and his biography. Unfortunately, it focused more on his professional career than the early years. Dan stayed up late trying to hunt down his place of birth, but he couldn't find that information anywhere with the search engines on his home computer. He would have to take the query to work tomorrow morning. So far, though, all he had learned was that Jack Stevens was born on March 12, 1970—and he did not believe in horoscopes.

It was Thursday, almost a full week since the latest attack, and Dan had yet to come across any living individual named Jacques in any of the family lineages he was researching. He froze Kristin, Boris, and Rachel out of his life, only making time for brief conversations with Chief. He stopped dreaming about Annie; now, he dreamed only about a shadowy figure named Jacques, lingering at the edges of every room. Dan was certain the killer hadn't had his fill of wine or blood yet. No matter how deeply he looked or how many times, he just couldn't connect the name Jacques to Jack Stevens, whom he'd finally surmised was from Texas—about as far from France as you could get. He knew how this individual was selecting victims and how he was murdering them, but he still had zero leads as to who, exactly, this killer was.

He went back to the drawing board, square one: Charlotte Hayes.

Dan exhaled deeply and flowed from downward dog into upward dog, exposing his chest to the sky. He thought of Annie, flowing beside him, as she always had, and this time, he didn't push the vision away. He let it take him over, let himself remember her in all her glory, and it hurt like hell. He curled into child's pose, pressing his face toward the carpet. A fuzzy old memory bubbled out of his subconscious. Annie knelt in front of him, a faded dream of a woman, and he stretched out his hand, running it along the notches of her spine. She had continued to do yoga until she no longer could.

"Annie," Dan said, his breath shallow, as he pulled himself upright and exhaled again, eyes still closed. It wasn't a hello or a goodbye, just an acknowledgment of her presence.

After spending two years pushing her away, like she was a scent desperate to be shaken, he was ready to give up. To give in. Just let her live here, inside him, for the rest of his days. He couldn't keep smothering her, closing the door when she would knock. As if the past ten years had just never happened.

That was the exact mentality that had led him to completely sabotaging his own recollections of their honeymoon through France and Italy, a time in his life that now gave him fantastic insight into his current case. He had to remember. If he erased the past, he erased himself. If he erased Annie, he erased himself. Did he really want to live the rest of his days knowing he'd actually died a long time ago?

Chimes went off through the house and Dan wrinkled his brow. He hadn't realized he'd just been sitting for a few minutes, lost in thought. It was late. Who was here? He looked at the windows in his bedroom, facing the backyard. The sky out there was a dusky plum, due partly to the setting sun and partly to the swell of pregnant clouds over his home. That was California for you. One minute, the soil was as dry as a bone, and the next, you were soaked in a five-minute summer storm, raging and then vanishing into thin air.

Slowly rising, Dan padded barefoot toward his front door, scouring his memory for anyone he may have invited over. No. Not today. If he had, he wouldn't have put on his pajama pants so early in the evening, and he would have prepared something to offer the guest. He paused just outside the foyer. What if it was another nondescript package, filled with wines? A basket of flowers and fruit? A little card that said, "*Bon appétit*," along with a gun to hold to his temple?

He crouched and tiptoed through the foyer, slow and silent. He had to open the door. He knew he did. He couldn't live in fear, or the killer would win.

But he could live in reasonable suspicion and prolong his probability of survival, couldn't he?

Through the blinds that hung in the front window, Dan saw the porch motion-sensor light—part of the enhanced security package he'd had installed after receiving the gift from the killer—had been triggered.

With a scowl, Dan edged toward the window and parted two veins of the blinds with a tentative fingertip, searching for a delivery person, the indirect and unknowing accomplice to murder, but the figure awaiting him was a sophisticated, solid gray queen with whom Dan had been in contact a few days before: Charlotte Hayes, connoisseur, author, and professor. Dan had left a message to which she had never responded, and he'd considered the matter laid to rest, but here she was, poised on his stoop in the midweek twilight, her gloved hands clutching a small snakeskin handbag. Everything about her was both petite and grandiose, from the delicate layer of lace fringe encircling the brim of her little pillbox hat to the tips of her tiny designer heels, a pattern that perfectly matched her snakeskin handbag. Her entire ensemble looked like it was worth a few grand at least.

Dan opened the door in a hurry, nearly giddy. "I didn't realize you would come."

"You were almost right," Charlotte replied warmly. "This is truly not my business, Detective Winters. I'm not that kind of girl, as they say."

"I understand, Miss Hayes." Dan bowed for her to enter, and she swept past him before he looked back up, so he saw her tiny high heels flash over the tile with a click, click, click. Her calves were wide and round without a single wrinkle, but her ankles were tapered to practical pinpricks.

"It's difficult for anyone to pass into my world," he said, helping her remove the black silky cardigan over her beige dress. "Most people leave as soon as they cross the threshold."

"Why don't you lead me onto your veranda instead, then?" she said. "Do you happen to have a mere thimble of sherry, my boy?"

"Right this way." Dan would do whatever she needed to loosen up enough to talk. She sauntered over to a patio chair and settled, crossing her legs. He brought her a glass of syrupy, strawberry-blond wine. She took a mild sip and offered him a smile, satisfied. Wine lovers may seem complicated to the outside world, but Dan knew you could tame most of them with their drink of choice and a good view.

He explained all the developments in the case since he had seen Charlotte last: the victims having all descended from families with a stake in a Richebourg vineyard; the possibility of a person named Jacques being involved. He knew his theory was close to complete. He was missing only a few pieces.

After he spoke, Dan asked Charlotte for any stirrings this tale might have given her, and she settled back, thoughtful.

"It's funny you should say that," she answered after a few moments. "There was a Jacques involved with the Richebourg plots—but he's no one recent. It's an old legend from some thirty or forty years ago, back when I was young, learning the difference between one grape and the next."

"An old legend?" Dan prompted, encouraging her to continue. Overhead, the clouds coaxed her on with a soft rumble. "I didn't realize the industry came with—what—ghost stories and heroes?"

Charlotte's eyes wandered over Dan's shadowy, sprawling backyard as though she could see every detail of the story laid out in front of her. "Jacques Durand is something of a wine-lover's ghost story." She bit down on her lip, which was painted in chocolate-colored lipstick again. "The boy was driven mad with wine."

"Oh. How have I never heard about this?"

Charlotte giggled loosely. "Oh, Detective Winters. It's a legend, you know. A myth. Few people know of it now, or ever even think about it, and those few are all—mature specimens, like me. You cannot find this in any book, and any teacher younger than fifty will likely have never heard it. But there was a Jacques Durand born in the early 1970s, as I recall. That is all we can know for sure. That is all one can find, supposedly, in actual print. The story itself is so much more, though. The stuff of wine tastings that run late on a dark and stormy night." She crinkled her nose and shook her head, leaning in conspiratorially. Fat droplets of rain pecked into the earth, but Dan and Charlotte were protected by the eaves.

Dan's buttocks teetered on the edge of his seat, almost painfully. "What happened?" he whispered, prepared for a juicy shiver.

"Young Jacques came into the Frantin family through marriage. He was just a boy, very small still, when Master Frantin married his mother and took him into his home. Master Frantin ended his own life a few years later. You know that the Frantin vineyard was once much larger and could have been very prosperous, but plot after plot was chiseled out from under him. The rumor is that the father Frantin left a suicide note that blamed the other plot owners for slowly whittling away at his property."

"Oh, wow," Dan said. "How tragic."

"It was said that the boy took it even worse than his mother, who had a beautiful face and a small heart. Master Frantin had become the father Jacques never had, even though there was no formal adoption or anything of that sort. The story goes that young Jacques was the one who discovered Master Frantin's body down in the cellars. In fact, he spent the night lying with the body, they say. They also say when he discovered his dead father, the madness began. It began slowly, you know. He was still very young."

In the distance, a bright flicker lanced through the storm clouds, causing Dan to jolt. "Imagine," Charlotte continued, "finding the dead body of a person you've come to love so dearly."

Dan didn't tell her that he didn't need to imagine it. He knew that moment. He could feel it under his skin, how the room had spun when his eyes first lit across Annie's body sprawled on the living room floor. He didn't have to imagine how it felt to find the body of someone you loved who had died by suicide. His heart stretched back into history, and he felt close to the killer again. At least he'd been an adult when he'd found Annie's body. It would have shattered the psyche of a small boy like that.

"The mother found them both in the wine cellar the next morning," Charlotte went on, ignorant to the poignant moment Dan was having. "He had spent the night sleeping beside Master Frantin, covered in his blood. The man, they say, had slit his wrists with one of the wine bottles. The police could hardly differentiate between the blood and the wine staining the cellar floor. Now, the woman, the mother, she inherited the Frantin vineyard, as a legal spouse, but that didn't mean anything for her son, who had never been formally adopted. In some ways, she seemed happy, they said—but she was also on the brink of madness herself. Her beloved was dead, and she was alone in the vineyard. There was only herself and her son, and she had never been the maternal type. When Master Frantin died, she lost what sliver of humanity she had left, and began to abuse the boy in most horrible ways."

The sky was fully dark now, but the rain had abated. A strong, earthy wind blew, rich with water and dirt.

"What did she do?" Dan whispered, afraid to hear the answer. He didn't want to feel any more sympathy for this psychopath than he already did, but Miss Hayes was not making it easy for him to remain unmoved.

"Jacques was locked in the wine cellar for days at a time without food," Charlotte whispered back. "We don't know where she went at these times. Perhaps she was there, or perhaps she completely abandoned the vineyard, but the legend goes that Jacques survived on his wits alone, smashing and drinking the cellared wines to get by, turning over stones in the cellar floor for whatever insect life could sustain him until he could be rescued. And he was rescued, but not soon enough. The boy was apparently driven mad with wine. He depended on it, romanticized it, and loved it in replacement of Master Frantin. They say he was something of a prodigy, as if he understood the soul of the grapes—but, in exchange, the alcohol robbed his humanity."

"My God. How horrific. Did the mother ever come back?"

"She did," Charlotte said. "She did come back—to the waiting cuffs of the French authorities. She was placed into jail for some amount of time for neglect, but the maintenance of the land, and her son, of course, were lost to her. He became a ward of the state, they say, and that is where the trail runs cold. Being born in 1970s, Jacques Durand might still be out there, of course. He would be, let's see—"

"Fifty-two, if he was born exactly in 1970," Dan said. "Do you think he could have been adopted by an American family?"

"I don't see why not. He could be in an institution now, of course. That is what I would expect—if the story is even half true!" she said with a playful swat at his hand. "Master Frantin, slitting his own wrist with smashed wine bottles? Come on now. Some of this simply must be fiction. It's so impractical."

Dan nodded and swallowed. "You know, it's funny," he said with a nervous little laugh, "but Jack Stevens was born in 1970. And I couldn't find any information about him anywhere."

"That is funny," Charlotte said, grinning, "because I can't imagine a man less capable of murder, detective. You should focus your magnifying glass elsewhere."

"Oh, you know Jack?" Dan said. "I didn't realize."

"I was his examiner, actually, a long time ago," she confessed with a little smile. "I shan't dare say how long."

"Ah—so you were the one who gave him his failing grade."

Charlotte sat up straighter. "The boy did fail the practical. I was shocked myself. It only involved six simple wines, though I can see how they might be complicated."

Six wines.

"Six simple wines?" Dan coaxed. "How can you possibly remember such a small detail from so long ago?"

"It wasn't that long ago," Charlotte sniffed, though it most certainly was. "But I remember because the poor, sweet thing was very upset about it and begged that I look the other way. When I would not, he even lodged a formal complaint with my institute, saying that I was guilty of misconduct during the exam."

"And yet you defend him as a man incapable of murder."

Charlotte scoffed. "He was still a boy at the time—twenty-five or thirty. He can be excused. You know how those years can be before you've found your groove. They can be terrifying. Of course, Jack made his own way, and that eased my conscience. I knew that he loved wine, but I could not control that he failed to properly identify the Muscadet."

Muscadet … Kristin …

The salinity, Kristin had whispered back on that blustery, romantic night. *The high salinity reminds me of Nantes, full of marshes and high mineral soil. The melon de Bourgogne white grape tastes almost like oyster. And it's fermented on the lees, stirred with a dodine.*

The Muscadet had been the wine of Sean Mugneret's murder, undoubtedly the sloppiest and most violent of the six known to have been attempted so far. The one that punched an inexplicable hole in Dan's hypnosis theory.

"Do you remember the other five?" Dan asked, almost afraid.

"Ugh. Yes, I do, detective, though I think this information is truly useless. But that test portion dealt with the Muscadet, as well as a Riesling, Coonawarra, Northern Rhône Syrah, and a … a … " Her eyes searched the ether, like she might find the final glass there. "Well, damn," she muttered. "I can't remember."

"A Friulano?"

A slow smile of appreciation spread over Charlotte's face. "How ever did you know that? Shame that I can't recall it more specifically right now."

It was a shame indeed, but the information served well enough; there was at least one more wine to be served at the fatal banquet if Jack Stevens was Jacques Durand of the Richebourg ghosts.

12
BLOOD RED LIPS

Thursday felt electric with anticipation. Dan forced himself to go through the chore of paperwork rather than do the one thing he wanted to do: drag Jack Stevens down to the station for questioning. There had been the coincidence of Jacques and Jack, the coincidence of being born in 1970, and now, the coincidence of the failed exams. Oh, and the wines! How many coincidences did there have to be before evidence ceased to be circumstantial?

Still, he knew he wasn't close enough to justify a warrant. If he went to Chief with what he had, he might find himself removed from the case all over again.

But Charlotte's lilting voice kept coming back to haunt him.

Six wines.

If Jack was their man, another killing was on the horizon, and the murderer had never hesitated longer than a week or two. How long had it already been since the failed attempt on Simone's life? A week?

Each hour, more grains of sand slipped through the glass.

He called *SF Daily*, the publication that hosted Jack's column, and they informed him that he would be out of the office, on vacation for this week. Dan asked where he was going, but they couldn't divulge that, of course.

At the end of the workday on Friday, Dan could hardly contain himself any longer. Everything fit together so perfectly. He had to tell someone what was going on. He had to find out where Jack had gone on his vacation …

Dan realized his car was pulling into Kristin's driveway before he consciously thought of going there. He just needed to talk to someone, and when he thought of someone to talk to, Kristin's image cropped up.

Which was new to him. It had always been Annie's.

Dan advanced on the front door and only hesitated when he reached the stoop, realizing he had no idea what he looked like right now. What if he had some of the romaine from his lunch's Caesar salad wedged in his teeth?

Where could he find a mirror on the spur of the moment? Maybe his phone's cam—

The front door opened, and Dan's eyes swung up to meet Kristin's—caught. Oh well. So much for the lettuce that may or may not be in his teeth. For the first time in weeks, Kristin looked like a regular beautiful woman, and not some spectacular bombshell. Her hair cascaded down one shoulder in a loose ponytail. She was simply clad in jeans and a white t-shirt. She wasn't wearing shoes and her hands smelled of bleach and plastic. Technically, she shouldn't have been intimidating. She couldn't have been more average than she was right now—but she was still simply stunning.

"Dan," she said, propping one hand on her hip. "What are you doing here?"

"I—I don't know, exactly." That was honest. "I needed to talk to someone, and I thought of you."

Kristin nodded, but her dark green eyes were cool, and she didn't smile. Dan thought this might have been the first time he'd ever seen her lackluster, but he was also sure it had nothing to do with him—right? He had just caught her at a bad time, hadn't he?

"You should have called first," she said coolly. "I'm cleaning right now."

"Of course." Dan felt an uncomfortable constriction in his chest. What had he done to her to deserve this mood? He'd seen her in a less-than-perfect appearance before this. "Should I come back later?"

Kristin tightened her lips. Although the answer was clearly yes, she shook her head and grumbled, "No. It's fine. Come on in."

"How have you been?" Dan asked as he stepped into the foyer, slipping off his shoes.

"My week has been fine." Her tone was curt as she led him back to the kitchen. His eyes stung with the overwhelming medley of cleaning solutions, though he was certain that, to the untrained nose, the scent would be light. He hadn't realized a week had gone by since he'd spoken to Kristin last—the night of that wine tasting. Was that the reason for this mood?

"How about you?" she asked stiffly, snatching up a limp white rag and whipping it over the surface of the counter, which had obviously just been cleaned.

"I had Charlotte Hayes over the other night," Dan offered, hoping to massage this mood of Kristin's into something a little more receptive and manageable. "She sat down for some sherry, and we discussed Jack's history at her school."

That finally got Kristin's attention. "Jack Stevens?"

Dan nodded.

Kristin's brow knotted up. "Why?"

"Because … there was a Jacques Durand, born in 1970, adopted, but not technically, by the master of the Frantin vineyard. He became mentally unstable after the death of this father. Meanwhile, Jack Stevens, obsessed with wine, was also born in 1970, and I cannot for the life of me unearth any records of his birth."

Kristin stared at him now, crossing her arms in front of her chest. Her eyes were dark and flat with disappointment.

"You think I'm the one who's crazy," Dan said.

Kristin blinked slowly. "I didn't say that. I just think that Jack Stevens isn't. He's a friend of mine, Dan. I know him."

"Oh? I didn't realize that. How well?"

"We've attended some events together. I've seen him around town. I mean, I wouldn't say that he's one of my best friends or anything—"

Dan shook his head. "You aren't really friends with him, then."

Kristin visibly bristled. A fire leapt in her eyes and her neck tensed. "Don't presume to tell me who my friends are. I am his friend," she insisted hotly. "We were at the park together just a few weeks ago, but you couldn't come because you had to work. You met him, Dan. He's not a killer."

"You don't know anything about him," Dan said, tallying the facts on his fingers. "You don't know his family. You don't know his history. You don't know his relationships." With every point, Kristin opened her mouth, but Dan rushed forward with more words, and Kristin was forced to snap her mouth shut again. "You don't even know where he lives."

Kristin was seething. "I do too. He's in the Berkshire community, on that bluff overlooking the national park."

The flame of an idea sprang up in the back of Dan's mind and he pressed, "You have not," in the most crass, obnoxious voice he could manage, as if Kristin had never said an honest word in her life, "ever been to his house in your life."

"Oh my God!" Kristin cried, playing perfectly into his hand. "Yes, I have! The man lives in a red brick mansion. You don't forget a place like that."

Dan made a show of exhaling through his nose and nodding. "All right, all right. My apologies. You are friends with Jack Stevens, then, and I accept that you think he's not capable of murder."

"He's not. I'd stake my life on it."

Dan opened his eyes and looked at Kristin. Even right now, barefoot in the kitchen, her eyes wide with all the energy and rage of an argument, stinking of wood polish and household bleach, he still cared for her. "Don't say that. Don't stake your life on anything or anybody, Kris."

Reaching out to her, Dan tapped her on the shoulder, a friendly gesture of reconciliation.

"Dan—" Kristin blurted, but he had already shifted toward the door. When he turned back to look at her, she hesitated. Maybe she'd been about to say one thing, but now she chose another. "I'm sorry I yelled."

"Me too. I'll see you soon, Kris."

When Dan returned to the gleaming outside world and the piping hot sauna of his car's interior, he fired the engine up and stared at Kristin's home for a minute. He almost didn't do what he was about to do. He felt guilty using the information Kristin had given him against her "friend," but he had to know. He had to go. He'd never be able to get a warrant from Chief on such flimsy allegations, but there was bound to be an open window or a loose panel somewhere on that red brick mansion in the gated Berkshire community.

Passing through the gates of Berkshire was easy enough with a flash of his SFPD identification. Finding the red brick mansion was easy enough too, even though there were several; Jack's had a Stevens mailbox, predictably gilded in wooden grapes. There were no cars in the drive, but there was a two-car garage, and it was possible that anyone could have been there. But Dan assumed no one was, and that an advanced security system was in place, practically vibrating with sensitivity.

Dan skirted the property and scowled at the gate. It really isn't a mansion, he thought with some spite, refusing to define his tone as jealous. He approached the gate and stealthily climbed over it and into a picturesque backyard. His nostrils were overpowered by botanical aromas spilling together on his left, then whitewashed by an insane tsunami of chlorine on his right. Jack must have treated the pool right before leaving town.

With growing trepidation, Dan crept up the stairs to the sweeping back patio, painted a glossy, rich mahogany brown. Bees buzzed over the flowers, and the gentle churning of the pool filters made this all sickeningly suburban, to the point that Dan had to question his own instincts here. What was he doing? Kristin had already told him that Jack was no killer, that she'd stake her life on that.

It looked as if she might be right. Yet only a short while ago he was certain he was right. It seemed he couldn't trust his own instincts anymore.

He frowned and cast his eyes around the patio, seeking an entrance to the house, even though he was on the threshold of giving up altogether—then he went still.

One door was hanging open.

Who left doors open like that?

Dan swallowed and stepped forward. Someone was here. Or something had happened. He took every step in slow motion. Even scents faded into the background as the sound of his own heartbeat thundered in his ears. He stepped through the open door and into a plush living room.

The memory of discovering Annie's body just like this came flooding up in his subconscious, and again, he let all the pain and glory take hold of him as it unfolded. The same sense of disquiet had settled over him then, too. The certainty that something was wrong. Would he find Jack sprawled on the rug in another few feet?

But there was nothing.

Dan crept the length of the house and found nothing. Nothing …

Why would a grown man leave his home utterly defenseless, abandoning it to go on vacation? It didn't make sense.

Finding his way to Jack's bedroom, he pawed through the underwear drawer, thinking he might find a picture of a victim or … or something. But there was nothing.

He'd been wrong. He'd been wrong all along, and now, he was breaking and entering, a further wrong. (Well, not technically, even though it had been his intention.) He was the criminal here, not Jack.

He passed into the foyer, the last strip of square footage he had not yet walked, and paused at a small table in the entrance, the kind of thing a man might dump his keys onto when returning home from a long day at work.

There were two pieces of paper there, and Dan glanced at them without assuming they would be valuable.

His eyes bulged at the first slip of a paper.

It was a printed flight itinerary between New York City and Paris. Dear God, he had been in New York City—at the same time Dan had been there. And now, he was on his way to Paris.

Of course.

To the Richebourg plots.

To the last leg of land: the Romanée-Conti.

Dan shoved the old itinerary into his pants pocket and, almost as an afterthought, glanced down at the second slip of paper, a glossy, colorful square, some kind of invitation or coupon. His mind was too frantic with the success of his first find to focus on the content of the second piece.

Then he took a closer look. It was a laughing mouth, spilling wine—or blood. No, it was more than that. It was the profile of a young woman, laughing, gushing red liquid down her chin.

Dan crinkled his nose and flipped the paper over.

"DETECTIVE WINTERS" was scrawled over the printed text in wild, spiky penmanship.

Dan's entire body went cold.

Jack was in France, doing God only knew what, and he knew Dan was coming for him. He had known Dan would be here, in his house. He'd left the door open for him. He'd left the alarms off. He'd left a note. He had to be teasing him.

Dan read the invitation:

> Blood Red Lips,
> an exhibit by Phoenix Starling,
> long-awaited up-and-coming artist,
> at Downtown Heart.

THE EXHIBIT WAS OPENING TONIGHT. Dan's fingers swept across the glossy paper. He inhaled, shaken.

Why was Jack inviting him to this? Was it a trap?

He shoved the piece of paper into his pocket and flung open the front door, stepping out into the fading afternoon sunshine.

How long had Jack been watching him? How long did Jack know that Dan knew? And there was Kristin, protesting that he was her friend, that she would bet her life he was no killer.

What a mess.

✥

Dan burst through the front door of Downtown Heart and a dozen young faces swung to blink at him. The men were wearing things like Fedoras and delicate nostril rings, while the women sported masses of elaborately arranged braids and lipsticks in unexpected colors: black, blue, green. But it was Dan who looked out of place. He was the one panting and bright pink, the one sweating through his suit.

All around him were tables of glasses brimming with dark red wine. The clashing aromas made his vision swim. The artist had meant to create ambiance, he was sure, but all it was creating for his sensitive palate was one colossal headache. Shattered wine bottles sat on pedestals, just like the ones Frantin used to slit his wrists, he mused. Looming paintings engulfed the high, narrow walls of Sapphire's gallery—powerful, dark, expressionist works in black, gray, and red. Waterfalls of blood, or wine, and naked flesh laced in red droplets—his stomach churned.

Dan shoved down the nausea and pushed through the crowd, knowing he had to stay; Jack had sent him here for a reason. There must be something here for him. Jack was leaving him clues intentionally. The man wanted to be pieced together, to be followed, to be caught. Dan knew this profile all too well. The arrogance. The neediness. He should have seen it from a mile away. The man made his living as a critic, for God's sake.

Was it Phoenix? Was Phoenix Starling the person Dan was here for?

Dan hunted the young woman down at a sculpture composed of splintered, leaking barrels, chatting with a reporter about her creative process. The woman had half her head shaved, but the other half was voluminous black hair. She had a septum piercing and wore thick eye makeup in smoky tones of blue and silver. Her lipstick was bright, popping purple, and the rest of her outfit was all black. Without the visual chaos, she would have been quite pretty, but there was far too much going on for him to focus on her appearance. She stank of cigarettes. Menthol.

"Are you Phoenix Starling? The artist?" he asked, interrupting her explanation for how she had come to have such an intense relationship with wine. (Apparently, it was a big part of her experience studying abroad for her junior year.)

"That's me," Phoenix answered in a throaty, cultured voice that sounded more practiced than natural. She tossed her half mane of raven hair and appraised Dan with crusty lashes. "Are you a fan?"

"You could say that." Why not? Dan whipped out his badge. "I'm looking for any information I can find on a man named Jack Stevens. You know him?"

"Pfft," she scoffed, flicking her eyes up and down Dan's body as if showing him how unintimidated she was. This was, after all, her turf. She was surrounded by others of her kind. "You mean that tired old writer from the little San Fran column? Pass." She rolled her eyes and smirked. "Anything else?"

"He sent me here," Dan answered sharply, beginning to feel the strain of the ticking clock. He didn't have time to bother with this college girl's ego. "He seemed to think there was something I needed to see. Do you have any idea what it might have been? It's important."

"Sorry, man," Phoenix said, though she did not sound sorry.

"Detective Winters!" a familiar female voice called from Dan's right. He saw Sapphire Gianni, the gallery owner, weaving through the crowd. She was wearing an all-black cat suit, her waves of dark hair pinned into a tight bun at the top of her head. Pure 1960s. "Detective Winters—it's so crazy that you're here right now!"

"Is it though?" Phoenix replied, deadpan. She shifted back to the reporter and said, "Where were we?"

"Your summer abroad," the young man answered eagerly.

"Of course. Now, I had just met this Italian, this beautiful Italian, and he was …"

Sapphire slid an arm around Dan's and tugged him away from the blathering artist. "Someone left something here for you," she said. "I'm not sure exactly when, but I found it when we were moving all these canvases into the space for Phoenix's show. I put it into storage. It might even have been left here accidentally. Who knew you'd be here? Anyway, I've been meaning to reach out to you, but the opening made everything so hectic. It was wrapped. I didn't unwrap it. Maybe it's a gift?"

She had no idea how right she was, though Dan could assure her its arrival here was no accident.

He followed her to the back of the gallery, where she let him into a storage closet and sifted through an entire box of randomly stacked canvases and papers, finally extracting a thick, medium-sized frame wrapped in brown paper.

Scowling, Dan took the package and tore it open. He didn't have a second to spare or to worry about what Sapphire might see.

At first, the jumble of crude lines made no sense. Charcoal struck down a furrowed brow and smudges of thinning hair. Sad eyes. Sad mouth. Soft wrinkles were dabbed and dented on the portrait, giving depth and texture to the skin. The piece was unsophisticated, as far as art went, but Dan understood it well enough.

It was a man.

Judging from the size of his neck and shoulders, this man had a slim build, and his hair was dark and well kept. It reminded Dan of himself.

Or … it was Dan.

It was him.

Beneath the portrait were scrawled the words, "*Bon appétit.*"

Dan felt the blood drain from his face, and he tucked the picture inside his jacket. Chief would have to listen to him now. I mean, this was a threat on his life, wasn't it? Jacques Durand was trying to trigger him right now to kill himself, using some hypnotic suggestion safely embedded in his subconscious weeks ago and then forgotten. But when? He'd only met the man once … hadn't he?

Thanking a startled Sapphire with his parting breath—more of a grunt, really—Dan made a break for the exit.

13

PAID VACATION

He couldn't get the portrait out of his head, so he dragged Chief out of bed to meet him at the station. He couldn't relax, couldn't think, until that damn thing was safely stored in an evidence locker. Until then, his own piercing charcoal gaze was locked onto himself, like some haunted doll following him with its eyes as he moved around.

In the half light of the precinct parking lot, Chief looked grim and exhausted, and Dan would have felt guilty for waking him up if this hadn't been an absolute emergency (besides, it wasn't even eleven o'clock yet). Dan had wanted to go up to Chief's office, but Chief declined.

"That's all right," he grumbled. "We can do this here." He pointed forward, indicating that Dan should expose the evidence beneath a parking lot light.

Dan furrowed his brows at Chief's dismissive attitude. He figured this would be just like how he said Dan "forgot" he was in a "wine subscription club," which sent him all those wines. But a half-hearted, late-night audience was better than none, so he launched into a deluge of information he had kept hidden from Chief, including how he'd walked right into Jack Stevens's home and found the invitation for him, as well as the plane itinerary to Paris.

"I'm sorry I had to do it like this," Dan said, "but everything started happening so fast, and I couldn't wait another day, another minute."

Chief nodded slowly and rubbed at his mouth. "Uh-huh. Let's see it."

Dan brought the ghostly portrait into the light and Chief considered it for all of two seconds. "I'm going to tell you right now, kid, there isn't much we can do here. We'll have to wait until he returns to the country—if he does, Magic—or relay the case to Interpol. And that's if we can conclude that there is enough evidence against him that extradition is necessary. And I don't know if we have that much evidence here, honestly. I know it seems powerful. It does seem powerful. But it's all circumstantial."

"But you know—" Dan barked in frustration. "You know I'm right about this!"

Chief blinked, then shrugged. "I think you're right. But what I think doesn't matter. What matters is that your primary source of evidence was garnered through an illegal search and seizure, and it could still be circumstantial. This guy would need to get on the stand and confess to a jury and then persuade them to take this evidence seriously. Your name on an invitation to an art gallery opening? It's nothing, man. That's nothing." He nodded to himself and passed the canvas back to Dan. "Honestly, there isn't much here to go on. I don't think I could even rightfully enter this particular portrait into evidence. There's no reason to believe that a piece of art from the storage room of a gallery was intended for you, or as a threat."

Dan opened his mouth. How could this not be construed as a threat? "But the handwriting—" he sputtered.

"I'm not saying I don't believe you. There just isn't much we can do." Chief paused thoughtfully. "Except … maybe set you up with a liaison in Paris … if you wanted to finish off your vacation time in France this week."

Dan stared at Chief, not believing what he had just heard. Chief Lester Brigham had spent years eking out droplets of satisfaction by blocking every initiative Dan wished to pursue. Now, out of nowhere, when he least expected it and needed it the most—Chief was going to bend?

"You would do that for me?"

Chief shook his head from side to side. "You've been making serious gains on this case in the past month, and I—" He hesitated, then pushed forward. "—I believe in you, I guess. Just … don't screw it up." He offered his hand to Dan and Dan took it eagerly, giving a vigorous shake. He felt a surprising stab of remorse for how much negative energy he'd been sending to Chief for years. The man was a surly old dog, but he was all right. "I'll set you up with that liaison, you get the ticket, I'll approve the time." Chief concluded, "and you bring that son of a bitch home."

Knowing Jack was on the other side of the Atlantic Ocean, and having Chief's blessing on this case, a burst of renewed energy surged through Dan over the next twenty-four hours. He packed with a spring in his step, and a nervous uptick in his blood pressure. All his excitement could also be considered nervousness. Jack had written that trigger phrase for Dan twice; what did it mean? Was he a ticking time bomb? Would he even make it to France before he suddenly felt the urge to slit his own throat? And would he have the power to resist?

That was it—the reason Sean's murder had been so different than the rest. He'd resisted. The trigger phrase hadn't worked on him. Amanda, Branden, Raymond, and Simone had all succumbed. Sean hadn't, and neither had Dan—yet.

He watched his own every move as he prepared his home for his absence. In the kitchen, he kept his hands away from his knives, the gas stove, plastic bags. Upstairs, he steered clear of long falls and open windows. He would be okay, right? It wasn't like he had felt the inexplicable urge to spread dry rose petals on his bed or put oysters in a dish on his bookcase. He was okay, right?

Striding down his upstairs hallway with his carry-on packed, he hesitated at the guest room. Its window was open just a fraction. He swallowed. He would have to close that before he left. Rain could creep in and ruin the upholstery on the window seat.

Dan clenched his jaw and strode forward, gripping the window and then hesitating.

Did he want to jump?

He exhaled slowly. The deck below looked beautiful today. The flowerbeds were tended, and the lacquer was glossy and fresh. Wouldn't it be a fitting, poetic end? To crash to his own death only a dozen feet from where Annie took her life.

He took a deep breath and observed the thought, letting it run over the surface of his skin like a razor blade with no pressure on the handle. He let himself feel it … and then he let it go. He pressed his hands down, closed the window until it sealed and flipped the latch.

He wasn't going to try to kill himself. Despite the fear and paranoia, Dan knew deep down that the killer's attempt to manipulate him would fail. It wasn't that he was immune to the power of suggestion, but in the days before their deaths the victims had all communicated with the killer. There was no doubt in Dan's mind that these interactions laid the foundation for a successful trigger. Dan dissected his memory for a possible interaction with

Jack that could theoretically be interpreted as potential coaching, but hardly could he have been that oblivious.

Even if there had been a repeated subliminal contact that he missed, the grooming seemed to work only on those uninitiated in wine. That's probably what set Sean apart, making him Jack's first failure. Could it be that, like a nefarious wine teacher, the killer set the trigger on those with a newly acquired sense of wonder? Everyone remembers that glass that started the love affair, how their senses awakened in that moment, giving rise to the overwhelming feeling of joy with life. Life has two phases—before and after the love of wine. Everyone has their own Château d'Yquem, Gentaz Côte Rôtie, Screaming Eagle, and life will never be the same after first sip.

With Dan being so different from the victims, why would Jack bother with him? Suddenly, the answer sent shivers down Dan's spine. If it was to scare him, then it worked. Jack was toying with him.

Dan had decided it was time to get a grip when he heard a voice.

"Dan?" Kristin interrupted his thoughts, and Dan whirled with a visible jolt.

"What?" he snapped. His eyes were wild; he hated surprise visits. People were always catching him at his worst while they were at their best. This was no exception: Kristin stood there with her green eyes, copper hair loosely curled on her shoulders, wearing a simple black suit. She smelled faintly of coconut oil ... sunscreen. "What are you doing here?"

"I ... I came to ... talk, I guess," she said, her forehead rumpled, and her mouth dented downward at the sides. "The last time I saw you—"

"Oh, I remember." Dan's tone was chilly. He swept past her, out of the guest room and toward the bedroom, where the large suitcase was open and almost completely packed at the foot of his bed. His flight was leaving in three hours, and he was the type of man who could plan for a two-hour cushion at the terminal and still somehow end up sprinting onto a plane during its last call.

"Did you ring the bell?"

Kristin's frown deepened as she followed him down the corridor. "Yes, I did. Several times. I was worried. That's why I let myself in. The last time I saw you," she continued, turning with Dan and entering his room with no hesitation, "I remember being kind of … distant." Now she froze, forgetting her sentence. "What's going on?"

"Chief Brigham set me up with a liaison in France," he told her, clapping his suitcase shut and zipping it. "I'm leaving tonight."

Kristin didn't respond, and when Dan looked up from his suitcase, he saw her fluttering her eyelashes in a way that would have seemed dramatic to someone who didn't know her. But Dan knew that the way Kristin carried herself was no manipulation. She was just in shock, she wasn't flirting.

"I—I don't—what happened?"

"To make a long story short, I procured some evidence that convinced him." Dan took a small, vindictive measure of satisfaction in being unable to tell her about his discoveries, because she didn't have faith in him when he brought Jack before her as a suspect.

"Jack is in Paris, and I'm following him." He hesitated and couldn't resist making a self-righteous jab: "You're not going to tell him, are you? Since you two are good friends?"

Kristin opened her mouth with surprise and then clapped it shut again. "No," she finally said. "I'm not."

Dan picked up the suitcase and carried it out into the upstairs corridor. "Good," he said over his shoulder.

"Is it going to be dangerous?"

"A little." Dan headed downstairs. "But I'll be fine. It's no more dangerous than San Francisco." He scooped up his carry-on when he reached the landing and then faced Kristin, offering a perfunctory smile. It didn't originate from a warm place; it was more of a social nicety. "I'd offer you a drink," he said, reaching for the knob and pulling the door open, "but my flight leaves soon."

Kristin nodded and swallowed. "Well," she said quietly, her energy becoming dim, which was strange for her. "Good luck, tiger." She hesitated before dropping the ghost of a kiss on his cheek. If he hadn't seen her do it, and felt an overwhelming wave of coconut wash over his senses, he might have thought it was just a breeze coming through the door. Her palm rested on his shoulder and gave a light squeeze. For two or three seconds, they peered into each other's eyes, and that little light he was used to seeing in Kristin rekindled.

"I'm sorry," she blurted. "I'm sorry I didn't believe you. You were right. I … I don't really know Jack. And … it's not even about knowing Jack. It's about knowing you, Dan. I know you."

Dan quickly stomped out the little spark that had spread from Kristin to himself. He didn't have time to think about that. He had to focus. "Thank you, Kris," he said, and took her into his arms for a brief hug. She was soft and warm, and it took some control to pull away from her. Being with her, he forgot about the case for just a little bit. Being with her relaxed him. But still, he didn't return the chaste kiss. "I'll see you in a week," he said, closing the door behind them as they stepped out onto the stoop.

"Be careful," she called from behind him as he locked his door and told her he would. He heard her heels clicking on the walk and when he turned around, gripping his luggage in one hand, she was already pulling open the door of her car and slipping inside.

Dan grimaced.

He hoped she would be careful too. He wished he'd said that.

14

MY ONLY FATHER

Lieutenant François Bernard was waiting for Dan in the Charles de Gaulle airport Arrivals Hall when he finally landed early the next morning. He was holding up a sign that read AMERICAN POLICE. Not Detective Daniel Winters, but AMERICAN POLICE. Still, Dan got the message and waved. François was small and round, with a face that unfurled its wrinkles as he smiled. His nose was slim, his jaw square, and his eyes bright and incisive. Dan got a good vibe from him. He looked smart, and he smelled like nutmeg and coffee beans.

"Hello," Dan greeted him with a handshake, masking his surprise at the sweatiness of François's palm. "I'm Detective Daniel Winters, San Francisco Police Department."

"*Bonjour*, Dan." François returned his handshake with a little too much pressure and quickly took his hand back. "Sorry. I just had my third espresso."

"How would you feel about having your first wine?" Dan joked. The flight had been over ten hours in total, not including his layover at Dulles. It was eight in the morning, and he was only half joking.

The Frantin family home was a stately stone structure at the end of a wide dirt path surrounded by columns of grapevines. Midday sun cooked the dark leather interior of Dan's rental car, making the whole thing smell like a tannery as he bumped and jostled along the underdeveloped road. You couldn't find this kind of charm in America. Dan hadn't been to visit Richebourg for ten years or so, and he could feel it in his bones now that he was finally on its threshold again. Something like a long sigh traveled through his whole body.

He rolled the driver's side window down and let a warm breeze fill the car. It was pungent with bittersweet vines. Bittersweet. That was the perfect word to describe how it felt to return for the second time to the course of his honeymoon with Annie—but without her now.

The master of the estate, Albert Bichot, awaited Dan's arrival at the front of the house. He cut a willowy, towering silhouette against the uneven granite slabs of the manor's walls. As Dan pulled closer and parked the car at the front of the house, he saw Albert was holding a cigarette and glaring at him. He had cheekbones that looked carved out of stone, and a powerfully thin and crooked nose. His rumpled gray hair was thin, shaggy, and loose. Dan climbed out of the car and approached, also glaring. The sun was too damn high.

"Monsieur Bichot, I presume," Dan greeted him with a light bow.

Albert nodded curtly. "That's me. Hello, Detective Winters. Would you like a smoke?"

Albert brandished a tin from the back pocket of his taupe trousers and popped it open, sliding out a hand-rolled cigarette for Dan's inspection. Dan waved his hand at the offer. "No, thanks. Though I certainly appreciate your willingness to meet with me on this matter, even though, technically, it has nothing to do with you. It is possible Jacques could come here while he's in the country."

"Ah, I'm happy to help," Albert said. "If one of our ilk is truly committing murders, then I will do whatever is necessary." A smirk skirted the corners of Albert's lips. "He won't come here, though." Albert was somewhere in his seventies but had a wiry strength to his hands and arms. Dan wouldn't want to fight him, he knew that. Something about him seemed as if he would be capable of killing a man if he had to.

"I'm sure you're right," Dan said. "But I had to come back here. This is where it all began."

"Of course," Albert replied. "Allow me to give you the tour."

Albert gave him the official tour of the grounds, then led Dan into the house. They entered a long, narrow entry hall, a small sitting room, and then a sunny nook where Albert brandished a bottle of Frantin wine from 1979, quickly uncorking it. "This was the wine that was made in the year after Master Frantin's death. This is the wine young Jacques Durand used to wash down whatever unpleasant things he was forced to eat. Indeed, this is the wine on which he survived during his many periods of confinement, or captivity, really."

Dan swirled the dark, earthy liquid and waved it beneath his nose for a sniff. A dance of smoke and cocoa revealed itself to him and he closed his eyes.

"It is amazing how this one drink can change you," Albert said, watching Dan savor the notes of the berry. "It almost—"

Dan tilted the rim to his lips and allowed a sip to pass over his palate. He savored it as it moved through his mouth, imagining how Jack must have felt—to have been a mere boy, trapped for days, perhaps even weeks on end in a cellar of wines, forced to live off them and whatever else he could scrounge until he was worn down to his last ounces of fat.

Albert added, "It almost becomes a part of you."

"And for young Jacques," Dan agreed, "I believe that was especially true." He settled back in his chair. "Nine years old."

"Nine years old," Albert echoed. "A child." He tilted his head to one side like a bird. "It's difficult to imagine how he must have felt. A thing like that can get into a grown man's head forever—and much more a boy's."

"But you've hit precisely on the nature of my visit there," Dan said. "I need to understand Jacques—in order to catch him."

Albert took the glass from Dan and nodded deeper into the house. "Would you like to … walk amongst the vines?"

"I would like to see the cellar, if I may."

"Of course, detective," Albert said, stooping and sweeping his arm in invitation. "I see you have not brought a jacket."

"Yes, well." Dan furrowed his brow as he stood. "Is that going to be a problem? It's August."

"No, not at all. I just want you to be prepared. The cellars are very cold no matter what time of year or day it happens to be." As he and Dan walked, Albert shook his head again and muttered, "Jacques was just a child—a child."

"Did you ever meet Jacques Durand yourself?"

"Oh, of course I did," Albert replied. "Never for terribly long, but he was my nephew. My step-nephew, I suppose, though he was never formally adopted and the marriage … it was a short one. I only met the boy once or twice. He seemed … precocious. Sensitive."

Albert opened a thick wooden door that groaned with age. "This is the cellar where Jacques was kept." A chill, wet gust of stale air smacked Dan in the face. Ugh. He could already smell the old oak, the deep dirt of the earth, and the clammy stone wall. It smelled like an empty grave.

Descending the narrow stairwell with Albert, Dan was tempted to hold his breath, but he knew this cellar was going to be too expansive for him to survive the attempt. He shuddered as his feet hit the stone floor. Stacks of barrels spanned as far as the eye could see in either direction.

He couldn't imagine being trapped down here.

Especially a nine-year-old child.

No food. No bed. No toilet.

Another shudder ran down Dan's spine, and he was surprised by the way his throat swelled up with sympathy for the young Jacques Durand of 1979 —the same man who had been threatening him, stalking him, and murdering innocent people in the Bay area for the past month.

Dan paused to place both hands on a barrel. Forgetting about Albert, he slid his palms over the rough wood. In many ways, wine was like a man, like a mind, like a life. It began with only a seed of itself, but through a long process of maturation, something alchemical would occur, crafting a vintage that was sweet or sour, light or dark.

Dan took his hands away from the barrel and looked over his shoulder. Albert watched him expectantly, and Dan was stricken with a brilliant idea, which he also suspected was insane. "Would it be all right if I spent the night down here?"

Albert broke eye contact with Dan and surprised him by spluttering a little, clearly taken aback, although he must have seen plenty of things in his lifetime. A long pause ensued. "Well … I don't know … I suppose one night would be all right," he said. "You really feel that close to him?"

"As disturbing as it may be," Dan replied, "I do. We both possess this deep appreciation for wine and extraordinarily strong olfactory senses. We both failed our sommelier examinations, though he went into an unconventional career in wine, and I did not. We're close in age. And there's something about him—I met him you know. I know him as a man, today. The crazy thing was that I really liked him. I felt like we could have been great friends —in another life."

"I never would have expected that the boy who was Jacques Durand, the youth they called the 'boy driven mad with wine,' would one day work in the industry. I always thought Jacques was going to be an artist."

"Pardon?" Something about that didn't quite make sense to Dan. "I thought you said you'd only met him once or twice."

"That's true, but when I acquired the vineyard from his wife, I found that the cellars were filled with drawings Jacques had done. They covered the floors and the walls. It took the better part of a year to scrub it all away, you know, and there are still fragments here and there that I'm sure I missed." Albert sighed. "Troubled soul."

"Yes," Dan murmured, his gaze scanning the large cellar, which seemed small because it was filled with these racks of barrels. Small, and claustrophobic. He could only imagine what things little Jacques Durand had been driven to do to protect what few shards of sanity remained in his head.

"Won't you at least allow me to give you a pillow and some blankets?" Albert asked.

"The only thing I will allow you to give me is a bottle of wine. I want to get as close as I can to understanding how the boy was feeling as he was being driven mad."

Dan wondered if Jack Stevens was a clinical insomniac. Being down in this cellar, even just for the night, brought Dan's anxiety to such a high vibration that he knew sleep would be impossible. The air was too wet and cold to comfortably settle anywhere; just the thought of curling up on that icy floor sent shudders down his spine. Still, he stayed. Even knowing that, in his case, the door was not locked, he stayed. He listened to the wretched, dissonant, musical groaning of the water pipes as they heralded what must have been midnight and something scurried under another rack of barrels.

Vermin.

Dan tracked the shadow of a small, furry creature rushing behind a rack of barrels, and then it was gone, into some hole or up some ledge. His eyes flitted from the rack of the barrels and caught some surprisingly familiar white markings etched on the floor, almost completely hidden by the protruding ledge of an oak barrel.

How intriguing that the crudeness of Jack's artistry did not exceed his nine-year-old self, Jacques …

Compelled, Dan gripped and dragged the front corner of the barrel rack a few inches forward, exposing more of the childish artwork. It was such an asymmetrical jumble that he had to stare at it for several seconds until its rhyme and reason snapped into focus.

It was a fallen man, arms splayed into puddles of blood, surrounded by broken bottles.

Almost in shock with a kind of surreal appreciation, Dan glided his fingers over the long-forgotten literal etchings on the cold stone floor. Young Jacques must have been effectively gouging away the stone with something of his own, perhaps a knife or a large shard of glass. Dan traced the childish writing that was scratched into the floor alongside his portrait of his stepfather's suicide.

Romanée-Conti a tué mon seul père.

"Romanée-Conti killed my only father," Dan translated as he read aloud, breathing heavily.

He thrust the cellar door open and sent it hurtling into the dirt, then came pounding up the stairs. Dark sky and twisted vines spanned around him; the Frantin house was quiet. It may not have been midnight yet. Albert was sitting on the porch with a cup of something steamy balanced at his hand when Dan came rushing around the corner and running toward his car.

"I thought you were spending the entire night," Albert called to him as Dan jerked at his car handle and leaped into the driver's seat.

"Can't," Dan yelled as he turned the engine over. "It's Romanée-Conti!"

"What?" Albert hollered back. To Dan, though, Albert's shadow on the porch was already several miles away. His tires tore against the dirt and the driver's side door closed itself by the momentum of the car spinning and shrieking out onto the dirt path that would take him away from the Frantin estate house.

Dan didn't know where Jack was, or what he was planning to do, but he did know one thing: Jack was due to strike, and his target was the Domaine de la Romanée-Conti.

15
BON APPÉTIT

It was not hard to locate the sprawling rows of vines of the Romanée-Conti domaine but finding the main house and explaining himself to the master or mistress of the plot would be easier imagined than accomplished. Still, he couldn't let the same thing happen to this man or woman as had happened to the others in San Francisco. If he hadn't clutched his hunch and flown all the way to New York City, Simone would have died too. He'd saved her with only minutes to spare.

Dan reached the main house and parked. Every window was dark, but it didn't matter. There were no rules for this situation. It was possible that Jack could be here right now. It was possible he'd already been. Maybe everyone inside was already drenched in essential oils, corpses pickling in the humidity. Dan crossed the wide drive toward the main house and rang the doorbell with desperate severity.

Its sharp jingle chimed abrasively through the air. Jing, jing. Jing, jing.

But no one came to the call.

Dan rang again. Still nothing.

A curious burn tingled along the hairs of his nostrils. Dan flinched and gave another, more purposeful breath through his nose.

Smoke. Unmistakable smoke.

Dan sniffed a third time.

The rows of vines were not lit with the flame, yet he could smell it. He knew it was there, burning somewhere over these hills. It was certainly contained within the boundaries of the domaine.

Damn it!

Fresh understanding dawned on Dan one minute too late again: Amanda, Branden, and Raymond had established a pattern. Sean had broken it. Simone had broken it again. What if Jack was now improvising? If his attack on the Romanée-Conti vineyards broke the pattern yet again, this time deliberately?

Dan looked back and forth between the dark main house and the shadowy rows of vines stretching in either direction as far as one could see. He would need to follow his nose to find the source of the flame in time.

He ran toward the low stone barrier that stretched the length of the property, hurtling over it and cutting through the rows of dark grapes, his shoes pounding the dirt. Dan was forty-two, didn't smoke, and had been a runner for well over a decade. Even though he'd been less consistent since Annie's death, he knew he could do this. Every few yards, his pace would slow and his breathing would calm, even though his body was drenched in sweat. It wasn't from the effort; it was the sheer fever pitch of attempting to stomp out this lunatic. His heartbeat and the rasp of his breath echoed in tandem through his head.

Chasing Jack Stevens felt like groping in total darkness, the most singular of scents evolving into his only clues. If it hadn't been for his superhuman palate, he never would have made it even this far.

Dan hesitated and ran the vineyard air through his nostrils again. Where was the smoke now? Thinner here … he backtracked and moved to the left, where he struck the acrid odor again. It stung his eyes. He had to be closing in on it. It was almost unbearable now …

Dan scanned the vineyard. Across two hills of vines, a soft yellow glow kindled against the horizon. It was so subtle and dim, most would have assumed it originated within the imagination, or a fading sunset.

Just like the smell of smoke could have been in the imagination.

But not with Dan's acuity. He never imagined a scent.

The bonfire was still deep in the distance, almost on the horizon, but Dan had to go. He had to try. In a way, this was his fault. If only he had been faster, stronger, smarter. But it wouldn't happen again.

Dan launched off the ball of his foot as hard as he could and pounded down the row of vines, toward the unearthly glow flickering there. His heart surged in his chest and sweat blossomed at the small of his back and base of his throat.

It was the hardest run Dan had ever done. He was soaked in sweat and dizzy, barely able to breathe, almost on the verge of vomiting—but only seconds had passed, and that was the important part. Time was of the essence, though he wished the last thing in his system hadn't been a damn glass of wine.

He was closing on the backside of a small, red building, too small to be a home, and he loped toward the broad door, hanging wide open. The inside roared with a fantastic light and heat. It was only a matter of minutes before the flame would spread out among the vines and destroy hundreds of thousands of dollars' worth of property.

Dan could feel the heat pricking his bare hands and face from here. His agitated lungs gave up a spasm, forcing him to cough. He braced his knees and doubled over. Shit. If he'd had any cover, it was blown now.

A sudden force from behind him sent his body hurtling forward. The sky swerved overhead, and the earth crashed into his face. The sky swung forward yet again, and his head slammed into the trunk of a grapevine. Stars spun in his eyes. He was too disoriented to register the physical body of his attacker, though he vaguely knew it was Jack. The stature was correct, and the hair was the same, but everything was moving in a blur. Only Dan's instincts pushed his foot to Jack's chest, wedged it there, and heaved him into the air with all the strength in his legs and the leverage of the grapevine.

Time and space sharpened as Jack was catapulted several feet into the air. Dan's mind snapped into focus. Jack Stevens slammed into the backside of this barn—stable? carriage house?—dressed in black slacks, a white-collared shirt, a black suit coat, and a black tie. His outfit was appropriate for a wedding or a funeral, and Dan knew this was his grand finale. That was the dress code here.

Dan wiped the sweat from his brow and pulled in a cleansing, purposeful breath, even as its smoke strangled and died in his lungs. This was it. Jack crumbled onto the ground. The fire crackled inside. They were running out of time. Jack was caught. Adrenaline surged through Dan's system, tingling all the way down into his fingers and toes.

Clambering onto his hands and knees, Jack gripped one of the small, handheld tools lining the outside of the barn—a sickle. He tilted his head to the side and grinned.

"You have two options now, detective," Jack said. "You can become my inside lane to the San Francisco Police Department, or you can die here and now, among the vines. Kind of poetic, don't you think?"

As he said the last words, he raised the sickle high and wide over his head, angled down to slice into Dan. His voice changed as his abdomen tightened for the swing.

Dan saw the attack telegraphed from a million miles away, and he could tell such a wide sweep was easy to dodge. What was Jack doing? Playing? At a time like this? Did he even want to kill him, or was he only enjoying another game of cat and mouse?

Dan dodged to the left with a spin, but Jack let his body dip down with the momentum of the sickle, then swung it back upward. Dan jumped back and brushed against another row of grapevines. He jammed a foot into the trunk to give himself leverage and then lunged with a powerful right cross. It had been a long time since Dan had been in a dirty, cheap schoolyard fight, but he still remembered all the moves.

Jack took the hit, his head following the momentum of Dan's fist and going to the left. He staggered and his body fell open, defenses dropped. He held his sickle with a weak grip. Dan didn't want to kill him, of course. He wanted to bring him in—alive. He felt the power running in his veins, but Jack was huffing. He was about to keel. He just needed one more push.

Dan's hand darted forward and caught Jack's tie, dragging him into Dan's space and driving his foot into Jack's stomach. The other man cringed and sputtered, tumbling to his knees with his tie tight on his throat.

Still spluttering, Jack focused his energy and swung his sickle, snagging Dan behind the ankle with the blunt tip, pulling his leg out from under him and knocking him flat on his back. Dan rasped out a breath and stars swirled overhead. He hadn't seen the sickle hit coming and absorbed the impact with the ground, his body splayed. Dimly, distantly, a fire crackled. Time was running out. Someone here was going to die.

"Your choice, I guess," Jack said, still breathing heavily. His huffing silhouette loomed overhead and eclipsed the sliver of a moon.

Still with the sickle weakly in his hand, Jack swung it toward Dan's face. Dan felt his eyes bulge and dug his heel into the dirt, whipping to the left in a tight roll. The sickle embedded itself deeply into the dirt and Dan came up onto his knees. Yes! But the sickle came loose quickly and clocked him in the back of the head with its blunt side.

Everything turned black and fumbled away from Dan in a timeless place. When he opened his eyes, he found his hands bound behind his back. He craned his neck and shifted his wrists to determine that the material binding him was Jack's black silk tie. He leaned against the vine posts closest to the barn.

A surge of nostalgia swelled in his chest as he felt the vertigo of *déjà vu*. This was just like the dream that had plagued him on that night marking two years since Annie's death—the corpses on the vine.

The sky overhead was luminous with fire. It wouldn't be long before it crept into the vineyard now. Minutes. Two? One?

Not tonight.

Dan slowly worked the silk tie against the rough wood of the vine post. Jack sauntered back and forth in front of him, whacking his sickle into his palm thoughtfully. "You know, Detective Winters, I knew it would be you," he mused. "From the moment I first saw you, I knew it would be you. At that benefit banquet? Remember?"

Dan wasn't going to answer him until Jack said, "The one your dead wife used to always drag you to?" Dan's eyes jerked up to meet Jack's, stung by a real wound. His only real wound. "Shut up, Jacques!"

"Ah, the name of my boyhood. You have done your homework." Jack tucked the handle of the sickle into the crook of his arm and offered up slow, sarcastic applause. "Congratulations. A moral victory more than anything else, but a victory nonetheless."

"Why would you ever want a man like me chasing your stench?" Dan asked. He had to keep him talking as he loosened and unknotted the tie. He had to get his hands free.

"Because only a man like you would be capable of giving an exuberant, intelligent chase!" Jack jeered. "Look at how far you've come!" He spread his arms and Dan wished ardently that his hands were free, that he could stand up. Jack was wide open. Lazy confidence rolled off him in waves.

"I'm impressed, detective," Jack said with no small measure of sarcasm. "I'm truly impressed."

"Give yourself some credit, Jacques," Dan rasped. The motion of his hands needed to be subtle. At least his hands were pouring sweat. That made the silk slip. "You left me plenty of elaborate clues."

"Intentionally, of course. If I didn't try to give you a trail, we could never have met here. And what is the point of being the man driven mad with wine, if not to have a little fun?"

"Why me? I'm just a cop. What made you look at me, before you even knew anything about me?"

"I saw you at each scene," Jack told him. "How you could savor the bouquet of each death, while the other detectives just took notes. But you knew that the real clues were in the details." He drifted closer and stooped down on one knee, wielding the sickle, lowering his voice. "I knew you were the one. The only one worthy enough to follow me all the way to Burgundy."

Inside the barn, something snapped and crashed. A spray of sparks puffed up into the night sky. It wouldn't be long now. "Join me, Detective Winters," Jack said confidently.

Dan stared at Jack's sweaty, sooty face, and had no idea how to even comprehend what he'd just said. "Join you?"

"Join me! Yes!" Jack repeated, standing and throwing aside his sickle to give his hands a single, jubilant clap. "With the combination of your talent and my ferocity, we could burn a path through history!" He threw his hands into the air and turned his back on Dan, apparently forgetting he was a threat. He spread his hands in the air. "These bastards—the Romanée-Conti, and other massive, mediocre acreages like it—hold the industry captive!" He whirled back to face Dan again. "Don't you see what we could do if we refused them? We could liberate the entire region, Daniel!"

"Never," Dan spat. "I could never be like you." He glared up at Jack, making sure his face did not give away the silent victory of the tie slipping down his wrists, unknotted. "A wine, you will never understand, is the maturity of a fruit—not the destruction of its roots. You're not talking about bringing the industry to heel. You're talking about murdering it like it murdered your stepfather."

Jack froze and something happened in his dark eyes. They fractured. A roar traveled up his body as if it came from somewhere outside of him, and he charged at Dan with the full force of his frame, slamming into him and hooking his fingers into the other man's neck.

Dan slid to the ground and let his hands come free, but he didn't waste time clawing at Jack's hands. Even as darkness crowded at the corners of his eyes, he groped along the dirt for something, anything, a weapon. His fingers skirted over a rock, and he grabbed at it, but it was partially buried.

"Fine, detective!" Jack snapped. A fine mist of saliva sprayed over Dan with each of Jack's words. "Forsake your place at my right hand in the history books!"

Dan's fingers dug at the earth holding the rock.

"We could have become lessons in the sommelier academies of tomorrow, but fine. I'll go it alone. I'm only beginning," he promised. "You, stupid fellow, have no idea how good I will be! Amanda Leroy was just the start!"

The rock was almost loose. Dan wrapped his fingers around it and pulled it from the earth. Its edges fit his hand almost exactly.

"It's so simple, you know?" Jack said. "So simple. Do you know how easy it is to hypnotize a person?"

"Why don't you tell me?" Dan said, as much to distract his opponent as to fit the last piece of the puzzle into place. "Tell me how you embedded that phrase—"

But it was the sound of approaching sirens in the deep distance that drew Jack's attention, his eyes shifting from Dan to the tree line, and Dan seized the moment to swing hard at Jack's right temple. The rock struck him and sent him rolling, and Dan used the momentum to launch himself on top of Jack.

"Oh, Detective Winters!" Jack barked. This man had always held himself with such composure, but now, Dan saw the young boy inside him driven mad. "Don't pretend you aren't looking around every corner in fear of being hypnotized into your own suicide!"

Without a thought, Dan's fist balled and struck at Jack's face. Jack countered with a block, moving Dan's hand to the side, forcing his knuckles to pound the dirt.

"Ah, the matching suicides of Dan and Annabelle Winters," Jack half-rasped, half-jeered, gripping Dan's unbalanced arm and using the leverage to wriggle out from beneath him. "They'll be like his and hers towels."

Jack sprang up to his feet and sprinted to his sickle, snatching it up and giving it a tight series of swings in the space immediately in front of him. The gesture wasn't dangerous to Dan at all; it was clear he only wanted to impress or frighten.

But Dan felt hope spring up in his chest. A flurry of red, white, and blue lights was closing in from two hills away. Coming fast. Dan took a deep breath and calmed himself. This lunatic could sully Annie's name all he wanted; Dan was above the fray. He'd almost won. The police were practically on top of them now, and the fire—

"*Bon appétit,* Daniel," Jack yelled, whipping the sickle into the air, directly toward Dan's chest. He was going to kill him.

Dan spun to the left and the sickle buried itself into the right side of the stable, severing a weakened board of ember-chewed wood that clattered to the ground.

The sirens seemed impossibly loud—where were they? Too much motion, vines, and darkness—he couldn't see the lights clearly now.

Dan again spun directly into a combination of hits from Jack. Black, red, black, red, everything turned dark and bright again and again.

Unknowingly, Dan staggered progressively closer toward the opening of the stable. He heard another crash and fizzle from within. Were the vines still safe from the flames? He couldn't think about that now. He had to think about himself.

Dan's open palm flashed up and caught Jack's next jab directly. Jack was getting too confident, throwing less and less of his weight with each hit of the sickle; he was having too much fun.

Another jab sank into Dan's abdomen and doubled him over. His eyes squeezed open and closed. His vision blurred and focused, blurred and focused …

A sizzling, dazzling plank of singed wood fell right beside him.

Dan's hand flashed out, gripped the fallen plank of ember-chewed log, and flung it upward, striking Jack directly in the side of the face. His head twisted and he bellowed as he tumbled with the shock of the blow.

The sirens were deafening now.

Blue, red, and white whirled and screamed over them. Dan struggled to his feet and stepped back, intending to allow the French officials room to breathe as they descended on Jack. But he felt his hands wrenched behind his back and tight metal bands securing his wrists. Everything seemed suddenly muffled and far away. Someone was reading him his rights in French. With his various stabs, slashes, and pain, he couldn't focus on his second language and the words slipped away from him. He thought he might pass out.

An angry male voice broke through the crowd. Dan recognized it, and his heart gave up a weak song of relief. It was the voice of François Bernard.

"*Qu'est-ce que tu fais?*" François demanded to know what they were doing, coming to Dan and the officer who held him handcuffed. "*C'est l'inspecteur Winters!*" François clapped Dan on the back and cheered. "*Arrêté de faire le con et enlève ces putains de menottes!*" he shouted as the officer removed the manacles.

Jack Stevens, hands in cuffs, was dragged past under the sway of two other officers. The side of his face bore large blisters in a rectangular shape across his cheek from the final blow of burning wood.

He lunged toward Dan. "You should have killed yourself," he growled at the detective. Behind him, a fire truck unleashed its hose onto the fuming stable and drowned out the flames creeping onto the vines.

"You and Sean, just lucky," were Jack's last words as he was pushed into a police car.

16

BITTERSWEET

As the little wheels on Dan's suitcase bumped along the cement path toward his front door, he treasured this brief respite before Monday. Small white butterflies dawdled in the air over his flowerbeds—Annie's flowerbeds—in the sultry San Francisco twilight. Soon, too soon, Chief Brigham would orchestrate some sort of celebration on Dan's behalf. He couldn't even stand a paltry fifteen-second toast at the Leukemia Society's benefit, so there was no way he'd be able to withstand the pressure of being the centerpiece of an event.

But, for now, he was home. Where it was quiet. Safe. Where he could be alone with his thoughts. His wines. His Annie.

Dan hesitated as he fished the key to his front door from the other keys on his ring. This had been his second trip to Europe, but his first without her. She had always talked about how badly she wanted to see it all again.

Dan grimaced and slid the key into the lock, twisting the bolt away.

Then he hesitated.

His head rose and he looked behind him in a sudden, darting motion, somehow certain that Annie was right behind him. He could see her in his mind's eye. Her cheeks ruddy from a light sunburn during all the hiking. Flyaway wisps of blond curled on the crown of her head, like a halo.

But she wasn't there. It was just his sidewalk, his keys still clutched in his hand.

Yet he could smell her. He was sure of it. There was a subtle fragrance in the air, and it wasn't the strong, piney aroma of the hedges. It was as if a tendril of something had fallen just out of reach. It was her. Her scent. Lavender and vanilla and coconut and sweat. It was there, and then it was gone.

Dan never imagined a scent.

Had she been with him all along?

His crow's feet deepened into almost a sob, and he shook his head. His heart ached, but there was nothing he could do. Nothing he could say. He couldn't just stand in his front yard and talk to the hedges as if they were his dead wife.

Giving up a resolute exhale, Dan turned the knob. The front door of his home fell open and shadows rushed up from the ground like zombies in a graveyard.

"Surprise!"

Dan's eyes bulged and he blinked at the cheering crowd standing in his living room as if they all didn't qualify as home invaders. And they did. What were they doing here?

"Congratulations, kid," Chief Brigham boomed over the din. "You deserve it."

Someone flicked the living room light on, and Dan saw most of his office standing there—and Kristin. There was a damn cake on his coffee table.

"Do I deserve a heart attack?" Dan said, grasping the side of his chest and passing over the threshold of his home. "Do I deserve—" he silently counted heads "—sixteen counts of breaking and entering?"

"Damn straight." Chief grinned and clapped him on the shoulder, bringing him deeper into his own den. He hadn't had more than two guests in this room at a single time since Annie's passing. She'd always been the social one. "I can't believe you followed that son of a bitch all the way to France." He chuckled deeply and threw his head back. "And the French police tried to arrest you!"

"They read me my rights."

"That's not what I heard," Eunice said, laughing.

"Me either," said Juan.

"But Jack Stevens has been detained," Chief went on proudly, sounding like a father who was both shocked at and proud of his son's blazing success, "and will be extradited to the States. It's really quite amazing what that nose of yours can do."

Rachel Porter divided the room like a paring knife: petite and thin, but effective. Boris came crashing through that ravine after her, loud and broad.

"How did you do it, you—you, international man of mystery!" Boris cheered, smiling and enveloping Dan in a vigorous hug.

"I used to read his column every week, you know," Rachel added, horrified. "I had no idea."

"So, tell me about the final fight," Boris went on, shadowboxing in a series of tight jabs. "Did you get to say any badass parting words?"

"Not that I recall," Dan said, genuinely unable to remember. "There was a sickle involved, though, and that made things interesting. The barn was on fire. And at one point I had to slip my bonds."

Rachel gasped. "He had to slip his bonds," she repeated in a loud whisper to Boris.

"Well, man, when are we going to see you again?" Boris asked. "After the book tour, I imagine."

"Pfft," Dan replied, blushing. "This Friday, of course."

"Are you sure?" Boris said, raising one bushy, bristly blond eyebrow at Dan. "We haven't seen you in so long, I was afraid you forgot who we were."

"I could never," Dan said. "I was just consumed by this case, you know? But I'll be there on Friday."

Dan and Boris embraced again. That was when Dan smelled her.

Oranges and cinnamon. Delicate notes of clove and berry.

Kristin Meyers grinned and crossed the room toward him. She seemed to be moving in slow motion. Her dark green eyes never broke contact.

"You're back," she greeted him in her strong, throaty voice. She leaned in to hug him, but it was just a light embrace. It was little more than a touch to the small of his back and the ghost of her cheek, a few strands of hair beneath his nose. It was more than enough. He had missed her.

"I am," Dan said as she pulled away.

"Did you at least have time to taste anything?" she asked. Of course.

"I carved out a minute. How about you? Do you have a minute to spare?"

Kristin's eyes were lit from within, as usual, but there was something else in them now—a darkness, a sadness, that encroached around the light and threatened it. She seemed both happy and sad. That was it. "For you, of course," she said, and Dan felt relief spread in his chest. He gestured for her to follow him onto the deck.

"You look beautiful." He tried to sound casual. She wore a simple white sundress. No lipstick. Just leather sandals and sunglasses perched on the top of her head.

"Thank you," she replied. They stepped through the open glass door, and she settled uncertainly onto a patio chair, looking up at him with a small frown. "You never really gave me the chance to apologize for how I reacted when you told me you thought the killer was Jack."

"I did. You apologized."

"I apologized, and you heard it, but that doesn't mean you gave me a proper chance."

Dan nodded. "Fair enough. I suppose I just—expected you to trust me." He shrugged and leaned on the shallow wall of the porch rail. "I wanted you to trust me."

Kristin pursed her lips and stood. She braced Dan's jaw with the fingertips on both hands, and held that position for several seconds, just peering up at him. "I do," she said. "I did even then." Then her hands were gone. "I heard that the French police broke up a massive fight between you and Jack. The vineyards were on fire, and you were blindfolded."

"The vineyards never caught fire," Dan said. "I made sure of that. And I wasn't blindfolded." He shrugged. "I was just a little tied up."

Kristin threw back her head and laughed. "Leave it to you to downplay bringing a serial killer to justice alone!" She clapped softly as she giggled at him and took her seat on the patio chair again.

"Really," Dan agreed, nodding. "I thought for sure he was going to kill me at one point."

"Oh my God."

"He always triggered his victims with a simple '*bon appétit,*'" Dan explained. "And he's said it to me a few times now. I was positive he had hypnotized me without my knowledge. He seemed so certain that it was the ace up his sleeve, but it just didn't work. Nothing happened."

He glanced at Kristin again and saw her wide green eyes intent on him. He had to look away again. Sometimes Kristin was a little too much to take. "He said something to me as the police were hauling him off, though," Dan went on. "He said I was lucky. Me, and Sean Mugneret."

"I remember you telling me about him. The one at Half Moon Bay. The high salinity with the Muscadet. Bludgeoned to death with a dodine."

"That's right," Dan said. "I can't imagine what might be lucky about that."

"I can't either." Kristin's eyes were distant with thought. "He was the only one who didn't die by suicide. His trigger didn't work." She gazed at Dan with warmth and relief. "Well. Thank God yours didn't work, either. I guess not everybody can be hypnotized."

"I guess not."

"Well," Kristin repeated with a nervous smile. "I'm glad you got to have this moment." She touched his arm and rubbed it gently. "The conquering hero."

A small, sarcastic laugh slipped from Dan's lips before he could stop himself, even though he knew it was rude to deride Kristin's honest words. "That's not important to me," he tried again. "Catching Jack was important. How it gets played doesn't matter, only the outcome." His anxious expression dissolved away, and he settled easily onto the patio chair alongside Kristin. "But I did enjoy a change of scenery," he admitted. "And I feel … different."

Kristin nodded, raising her brow. "How?"

"Better. I don't know what it was. If it was being in France again, or just—living again. Taking risks. And I felt, feel, better."

He exhaled and let the tension run from his body before daring to say the next words in his heart. They were big words. "I think throwing myself into work has finally—finally—given me back some little piece of myself. I think this case dislodged something and I might be—" He almost didn't want to say it aloud and jinx his wish. At this point, it was a wish. It was a dream. "I might be able to move on—from my past. From Annie."

Dan had always hated the terms "move on" and "get over," particularly in relation to the loss of loved ones. It was such a dismissive way to talk about it, as if she was his first girlfriend and this was high school. But now that he'd spent the past two years trying to learn to live without her, trying to move on, he'd begun to understand the appeal.

"I still think about her all the time," Dan went on quietly, his eyes distant, although he could feel Kristin hanging on his words in the space just beside his shoulder. "But maybe I can still move on."

Kristin placed her hand on his knee and gave a squeeze. "I—"

The sliding glass door banged open, and Chief bellowed, "Here he is!" for the entire neighborhood to hear. "Where did you get off to, kid? We've got an entire precinct in one room, trying to hear this damn story already!"

Chief was in unnaturally high spirits, and Dan felt a chord of fear strike in his chest.

Maybe they'd gotten into his wine cellar.

"Is it true," Chief said, "that you were offered a movie deal before you left?"

Dan knew he was kidding, but still, Chief stood there patiently waiting for him to get up and come tell his story again, utterly deaf to the tone of the moment he'd interrupted. Dan gave Kristin a sorry glance and got up.

They filed back into the party and Dan fulfilled his obligations as the host. He told the story again and again. He shook hands. He thanked guests. He did it all, and at the end of the evening, when everyone had filed out into the night, high-spirited from the sugar and the alcohol, Dan dissolved into a puddle on his living room couch and didn't dare look around at the mess he'd be singlehandedly fixing in the morning.

"Ugh," he groaned, dragging himself into the kitchen for a single sip of wine before bed. "It's over. I did it." He half-filled a glass with a delicate, greenish-white wine—Sauvignon Blanc, Annie's favorite. He sipped at it and the tension ran off him again, for the first time since his moment on the patio with Kristin.

Was it strange that Kristin and Annie evoked similar feelings in him? It felt right and wrong at the same time. He shook his head only slightly and decided to discard the question as wildly premature. The glass was almost to his lips when he smelled it again for the first time since this afternoon: lavender, vanilla, coconut.

Dan whirled and scanned the empty kitchen, as if she might be there in her nightgown, looking at him.

"Annie?" His voice almost sounded like a beg. Of course, there was no reply. The house was quiet and empty, but he couldn't stop himself. "Annie?"

Still bracing his wine glass in his hand, he darted around the kitchen, literally chasing the scent, but never finding its origin. He pushed open the patio door and took a deep drag on the outdoor air. There was no hint of lavender out there, and slowly, slowly, the fragrance waned and vanished. Dan toasted the empty air of the outside world. "Goodnight, Annie," he called. "I'll be seeing you."

He brought the glass to his lips and sampled its crisp, grassy flavor, exhaling and opening his eyes to the humid, vast darkness of the San Francisco night, wondering where his old nose would take him next.

ALSO BY ACTON MANNING
VINE 45

A series of disappearances in France's winery region takes a dramatic turn when a dog sniffs out a severed arm among the vines. Summoned by a French colleague, San Francisco Police Department's Daniel Winters travels back to France, this time to the rolling, vine-covered hills around Avignon.

But the idyllic setting belies a simmering conflict: the old wine families, steeped in generations of winemaking tradition, resent the incursion of a young urban crowd who consider themselves the avant-garde of winemakers. The deeper Dan digs—and the more he learns about the global cultures and local cults that influence the French wine world—the darker the clouds seem to grow as they gather over the vineyards.

Can Dan prune back the vines enough to find the people who have disappeared? Or will this be the murder case that finally overwhelms the World's Greatest Nose?

SIGN UP NOW!

Learn about the fine wines Dan Winters enjoys in Acton Manning's novels.

Dig into the history of all things wine related.

Explore the world through the eyes of an author who's traveled its great winemaking regions.

Find out the next time Magic Man is on a case only the World's Greatest Nose can solve.

Sign up now for Wine and Crime, a newsletter for Daniel Winters Mysteries fans.

Just follow this link:

www.actonmanning.com/wineandcrime

Then pour yourself a glass of your favorite wine. We'll do the rest.

ABOUT THE AUTHOR

Acton Manning is a certified sommelier and international wine educator (Diplomate of WSET). Trained in emergency medicine, he's swapped his stethoscope for a virtual pen to create the Daniel Winters series. When he's not visiting the world's great vineyards or teaching fellow Dionysians how to enjoy fine food paired with wine, he can be found at his desk, working on his next Daniel Winters mystery while sipping a glass of his latest favorite muse.

www.actonmanning.com
@actonmanning
Acton Manning
acton.manning@gmail.com

YFB Publishing

 @ActonManning

 Acton Manning

www.actonmanning.com
acton.manning@gmail.com

Made in United States
Troutdale, OR
03/20/2024

18614442R00141